PRINCE
of
DARKNESS

& OTHER STORIES

PRINCE
of
DARKNESS

& OTHER STORIES

J. F. Powers

VINTAGE BOOKS
A Division of Random House
New York

To Chuck and Kerker
in gratitude

First Vintage Books Edition, October 1979

Library of Congress Cataloging in Publication Data
Powers, James Farl, 1917–
Prince of Darkness and other stories.
Reprint of the 1947 ed. published by
Doubleday, New York.
I. Title.
PZ3.P8743Pr 1979   [PS3531.084]   813'.5'4   79-7459
ISBN 0-394-74137-4

Manufactured in the United States of America

Contents

PRINCE
of
DARKNESS

& OTHER STORIES

The Lord's Day

The trees had the bad luck to be born mulberry and to attract bees. It was not the first time, Father said, and so you could not say he was being unfair. It was, in fact, the second time that a bee had come up and stung him on the front porch. What if it had been a wasp? How did he know it was one of the mulberry bees? He knew. That was all. And now, Sister, if you'll just take the others into the house with you, we'll get down to work. She had ordered the others into the convent, but had stayed to plead privately for the trees. The three big ones must go. He would spare the small one until such time as it grew up and became a menace.

Adjusting the shade, which let the sun through in withered cracks like the rivers on a map, she peeked out at the baking schoolyard, at the three trees. Waves of heat wandered thirstily over the pebbles, led around by the uncertain wind. She could see the figure of Father walking the heat waves, a fat vision in black returning to the scene of the crime, grabbing the axe away from the janitor. . . . Here, John, let me give her the first lick! . . . And so, possibly fancying himself a hundred years back, the most notable person at the birth of a canal or railroad, and with the children for his amazed audience, he had dealt the first blow. Incredible priest!

She left the room and went downstairs. They were waiting in the parlor. She knew at a glance that one was missing. Besides herself, they were twelve—the apostles. It was the kind of joke they could appreciate, but not to be carried too far, for then one of them must be Judas, which was not funny. In the same way she, as the leader of the apostles, feared the implication as blasphemous. It was not a very good joke for the convent, but it was fine to tell lay people, to let them know there was life there.

She entered the little chapel off the parlor. Here the rug was thicker and the same wide-board floor made to shine.

She knelt for a moment and then, genuflecting in the easy, jointless way that comes from years of it, she left. Sister Eleanor, the one missing, followed her into the parlor.

"All right, Sisters, let's go." She led them through the sagging house, which daily surpassed itself in gloominess and was only too clean and crowded not to seem haunted, and over the splintery floor rising and sinking underfoot like a raft. She opened the back door and waited for them to pass. She thought of herself as a turnkey releasing them briefly to the sun and then to their common, sudden doom. They proceeded silently across the schoolyard, past the stumps bleeding sap, the bright chips dirtying in the gravel, a few twigs folded in death.

Going under the basketball standards she thought they needed only a raven or two to become gibbets in the burning sun. A pebble lit in the lacings of her shoe. She stopped to free it. She believed she preferred honest dust to manufactured pebbles. Dust lent itself to philosophizing and was easier on the children's knees.

They climbed the cement steps, parting the dish towels on the porch as portieres, and entered the rectory. The towels were dry and the housekeeper would be gone. She sensed a little longing circulate among the sisters as they filed into the kitchen. It was all modern, the *after* for the *before* they would always have at the convent. She did not care for it, however. It hurt the eyes, like a field of sunny snow. A cockroach turned around and ran the other way on the sink. At least he was not modern.

The dining room was still groggy from Sunday dinner. They drew chairs up to the table in which the housekeeper had inserted extra leaves before taking the afternoon off. The table was covered with the soiled cloth that two of them would be washing tomorrow. They sighed. There, in the middle of the table, in canvas sacks the size of mailbags, were the day's three collections, the ledgers and index cards for recording individual contributions. They sat down to count.

With them all sitting around the table, it seemed the time for her to pray, "Bless us, O Lord, and these Thy gifts . . ."

Sister Antonia, her assistant, seized one of the sacks and emptied it out on the table. "Come on, you money-changers, dig in!" Sister Antonia rammed her red hands into the pile and leveled it off. "Money, money, money."

"Shall we do what we did last week?" asked Sister Florence. She looked hopefully at Sister Antonia.

"Cubs and White Sox?" said Sister Antonia. "O.K., if it'll make you happy." Sister Antonia dumped out the other sack. The winner would be the one counting the most money. They chose up sides and changed seats accordingly, leaving Sister Antonia and herself to do the envelopes.

Sister Louise and Sister Paula, who could remember several regimes before hers and might have been mothers superior themselves, constituted a resistance movement, each in her fashion. Sister Louise went to sleep in a nice, unobtrusive way, chin in wimple. But Sister Paula—Sister Cigar Box to the children, with whom she was *not* a great favorite —stayed awake to grumble and would touch only the coins that appeared old, foreign, or very new to her. She stared long and hard at them while Sister Louise dozed with a handful of sweaty nickels.

It was their way of informing everyone of their disapproval, of letting her know it had not been like this in former times, that Sunday had been a day of rest under other leadership. They were right, she knew too well, and was ashamed that she could not bring herself to make a stand against Father. Fortunately, the two old sisters could not carry the resistance beyond themselves. She left them to Sister Antonia. The others, to make the contest even, divided the dead weight between them. The Cubs got Sister Louise and Sister Paula went with the White Sox.

A horn tooted out in front of the rectory, and from his room upstairs young Father shouted, "*Cominnggg!* Tell him I'm coming!" The shout sailed down the stairway and out to Father on the porch.

"He's coming," Father called to the car. "How's your health?"

She could not catch the reply for the noise young Father made running around upstairs. He had on his shower clogs and was such a heavy man.

Finally the ceiling settled, and young Father came clattering down the front stairs, dragging his golf clubs behind him. He spoke to Father on the porch.

"Want me home for Devotions, Father?"

"Oh hell, Bill, have a good time. Won't anybody come in weather like this but the nuns. I'll handle it."

"Well—thanks, Boss."

"Look out for that nineteenth hole; that's all I got to say. Have a good time."

"You talked me into it."

Sister Cigar Box dropped a half dollar from an unnecessary height and listened to the ring. "Lead! And I suppose that was that Father O'Mammon in his new machine out waking the dead! I'm on to him. I had him in school."

"O'Hannon, Sister," corrected Sister Antonia.

"Of St. Judas's parish. I know."

"Of St. Jude's, Sister."

"Crazy!"

Father's radio woke up with a roar.

"The symphony!" breathed Sister Charlotte, who gave piano lessons to beginners six days a week.

"It's nice," Sister Cigar Box rasped when Father dialed away from it. "Wasn't it?"

Now Father was getting the news and disputing with the commentator. "Like hell you say!" Father had the last word and strode into the dining room with his collar off, bristling.

"Good afternoon, Father!" they all sang out.

"We'll have to fight Russia," he said, plunging into the kitchen. She heard him in the refrigerator and could tell that, rather than move things, he squeezed them out. He passed through the dining room, carrying a bottle of beer and a glass.

"Hot," he said to nobody.

The radio came on again. Father listened to an inning of the ball game. "Cubs are still in second place!" he shouted back to them.

"Thank you, Father," said Sister Florence involuntarily.

Sister Cigar Box said, "Humph!"

Now she could tell from the scraping noises that Father was playing himself a game of checkers. Periodically the moves became more rapid, frenzied, then triumphant. He was winning every game.

She asked Sister Eleanor how the map was coming.

"All in except Rhode Island and Tennessee. I don't know what's keeping them." They all knew Sister Eleanor was putting together a map from free road maps she got from the oil companies. She had been unable to get an appropriation from Father for a new one. He said they had a map already and that he had seen it a few years back. She had tried to tell him it was too old and blurry, that Arizona and Oklahoma, for instance, had now been admitted to the Union. Who cares about them? said Father. Give the kids a general idea—that's all you can do in the grades. Same as you give them catechism. You'd have them all studying Saint Thomas in the Latin.

"How big's it now?" asked Sister Antonia.

"Enormous. We'll have to put it up in sections, I guess. Like the Eastern states, the Middle Atlantic, and so on."

"You could hang it in the gym."

"If Father moved out his workshop."

"Some of the maps don't dovetail when they come from different companies. But you get detail you wouldn't get in a regular map. It's just awkward this way."

Father appeared in the door of the dining room. "How's she look?"

"More envelopes this week, Father," said Sister Antonia.

"Guess that last blast got them. How's the hardware department?"

Three sisters saw each other about to speak, gulped, and said nothing. "It's better, isn't it, Sisters?" inquired Sister Antonia.

"Yes, Sister."

Father came over to the table. "What's this?" He picked up a Chinese coin with a hole in it that Sister Cigar Box had been glad to see earlier. "Well, we don't get so many buttons nowadays, do we?" Father's fingers prowled the money pile sensitively.

"No, Father," said Sister Florence. "One last week, one today." She looked like a small girl who's just spoken her piece.

"One again, huh? Have to tell the ushers to bear down. Here, Sister, you keep this." Father gave the Chinese coin to Sister Cigar Box. "For when you go on the missions."

Sister Cigar Box took the coin from him and said nothing—about the only one not smiling—and put it down a trifle hard on the table.

Father went over to the buffet. "Like apples? Who wants an apple?" He apparently expected them to raise their hands but did not seem disappointed when no one did. He placed the bowl on the table for them. Three apples on top were real, but the ones underneath were wax and appeared more edible. No one took an apple.

"Don't be bashful," Father said, straying into the kitchen.

She heard him in the refrigerator again.

In a moment he came out of the kitchen with a bottle of beer and a fresh glass, passed quickly through the room, and, hesitating at the door, turned toward them. "Hot weather," he said. "Makes you sleepy. That's all I got to say." He left them for the porch.

The radio went on again. He had the Catholic Hour for about a minute. "Bum speaker," he explained while dialing. "Else I'd keep it on. I'll try to get it for you next week. They're starting a new series."

"Yes, Father," said Sister Florence, not loud enough to be heard beyond the table.

Sister Cigar Box said, "Humph!"

Father could be heard pouring the beer.

Next he got "The Adventures of Phobe Smith, the Phantom Psychiatrist." It was better than the ball game and news.

But Phobe, if Muller wasn't killed in the plane crash and Mex was really working for British Intelligence, tell me how the heck could Colonel Barnett be a Jap spy and still look like—uh—the real Colonel Barnett? Plastic surgery. Plastic surgery—well, I never! Plus faricasalicasuki. Plus farica—what! Faricasalicasuki—a concentrate, something like our penicillin. And you knew all the time——! That Colonel Barnett's wife, Darlene, was not . . . unfaithful? Yes! I'm afraid so. Whew!

An organ intervened and Father turned off the radio.

She recorded the last contribution on the last index card. The money was all counted and wrapped in rolls for the bank. The White Sox had won. She told them to wait for her and ventured out on the porch, determined to make up for the afternoon, to show them that she knew, perhaps, what she was doing.

"Father"—he was resting in an orange-and-green deck chair—"I wonder if you could come and look at our stove."

Father pried his legs sideways, sat up, and rubbed his eyes. "Today? *Now?*"

She nodded dumbly and forced herself to go through with it. "It's smoking so we can't use it at all." She was ready, if necessary, to mention the old sisters who were used to hot tea.

Father massaged his bald head to rouse himself. He wrinkled the mottled scalp between his hands and it seemed to make a nasty face at her. "Let's go," he said. Evidently he had decided to be peppy—an example to her in time of adversity. He scooped his collar off the radio and let it snap to around his neck. He left it that way, unfastened.

"Father is going to look at the stove," she told them in the dining room. They murmured with pleasure.

Father went first, a little unsteady on stiff legs, not waiting for them. He passed the stumps in the yard with satisfaction, she thought. "Whyn't you ask John to look at it yesterday?" he demanded over his shoulder.

She tried to gain a step on him, but he was going too fast, wobbling in a straight line like a runaway trolley. "I thought you'd know more about it, Father," she lied, ashamed that the others could hear. John, looking at it, had shaken his head.

"Do we need a new one, John?"

"If you need a stove, Sister, you need a new one."

Father broke into their kitchen as into a roomful of assassins, and confronted the glowering hulk of iron that was their stove. "Is it dirty or does it just look that way?"

She swallowed her temper, but with such bad grace there was no merit in it, only design. She gave the others such a terrible frown they all disappeared, even Sister Antonia.

Father squinted to read the name on the stove. "That stove cost a lot of money," he said. "They don't make them like that any more." He slapped the pipe going up and through the side of the wall. He gave the draft regulator a twist.

He went to the window and peered out. When he turned around he had the print of the screen on his nose. She would not say anything to distract him. He seemed to be thinking. Then he considered the stove again and appeared to have his mind made up. He faced her.

"The stove's all right, Sister. It won't draw properly, is all."

"I know, Father, but——"

"That tree," he said, pointing through the wall at the small tree which had been spared, "is blocking the draft. If you want your stove to work properly, it'll have to come down. That's all I got to say."

He squinted to read the name on the stove again.

She felt the blood assembling in patches on her cheeks. "Thank you, Father," she said, and went quickly out of the kitchen, only wanting to get upstairs and wash the money off her hands.

The Trouble

Neither the slavers' whip nor the lynchers' rope nor the bayonet could kill our black belief.—Margaret Walker, *For My People.*

We watched at the window all that afternoon. Old Gramma came out of her room and said, "Now you kids get away from there this minute." And we would until she went back to her room. We could hear her old rocking chair creak when she got up or sat down, and so we always ran away from the window before she came into the room to see if we were minding her good or looking out. Except once she went back to her room and didn't sit down, or maybe she did and got up easy so the chair didn't creak, or maybe we got our signals mixed, because she caught us all there and shooed us away and pulled down the green shade. The next time we were real sure she wasn't foxing us before we went to the window and lifted the shade just enough to peek out.

It was like waiting for rats as big as cats to run out from under a tenement so you could pick them off with a .22. Rats are about the biggest live game you can find in ordinary times and you see more of them than white folks in our neighborhood—in ordinary times. But the rats we waited for today were white ones, and they were doing most of the shooting themselves. Sometimes some coloreds would come by with guns, but not often; they mostly had clubs. This morning we'd seen the whites catch up with a shot-in-the-leg colored and throw bricks and stones at his black head till it got all red and he was dead. I could still see the wet places in the alley. That's why we kept looking out the window. We wanted to see some whites get killed for a change, but we didn't much think we would, and I guess what we really expected to see was nothing, or maybe them killing another colored.

There was a rumpus downstairs in front, and I could

hear a mess of people tramping up the stairs. They kept
on coming after the second floor and my sister Carrie, my
twin, said maybe they were whites come to get *us* because
we saw what they did to the shot-in-the-leg colored in the
alley. I was scared for a minute, I admit, but when I heard
their voices plainer I knew they were coloreds and it was
all right, only I didn't see why there were so many of them.

Then I got scared again, only different now, empty scared
all over, when they came down the hall on our floor, not
stopping at anybody else's door. And then there they were,
banging on our door, of all the doors in the building. They
tried to come right on in, but the door was locked.

Old Gramma was the one locked it and she said she'd
clean house if one of us kids so much as looked at the knob
even, and she threw the key down her neck somewhere. I
went and told her that was our door the people were pounding on and where was the key. She reached down her neck
and there was the key all right. But she didn't act much like
she intended to open the door. She just stood there staring
at it like it was somebody alive, saying the litany to the
Blessed Virgin: *Mère du Christ, priez pour nous, Secours
des chrétiens, priez* . . . Then all of a sudden she was
crying; tears were blurry in her old yellow eyes, and she
put the key in the lock, her veiny hands shaking, and un-
locked the door.

They had Mama in their arms. I forgot all about Old
Gramma, but I guess she passed out. Anyway, she was on
the floor and a couple of men were picking her up and a
couple of women were saying, "Put her here, put her there."
I wasn't worried as much about Old Gramma as I was about
Mama.

A bone—God, it made me sick—had poked through the
flesh of Mama's arm, all bloody like a sharp stick, and
something terrible was wrong with her chest. I couldn't look
any more and Carrie was screaming. That started me crying. Tears got in the way, but still I could see the baby, one
and a half, and brother George, four and a half, and they
had their eyes wide-open at what they saw and weren't crying a bit, too young to know what the hell.

They put Old Gramma in her room on the cot and closed

the door on her and some old woman friend of hers that kept dipping a handkerchief in cold water and laying it on Old Gramma's head. They put Mama on the bed in the room where everybody was standing around and talking lower and lower until pretty soon they were just whispering.

Somebody came in with a doctor, a colored one, and he had a little black bag like they have in the movies. I don't think our family ever had a doctor come to see us before. Maybe before I was born Mama and Daddy did. I heard the doctor tell Mr. Purvine, that works in the same mill Daddy does, only the night shift, that he ought to set the bone, but honest to God he thought he might as well wait, as he didn't want to hurt Mama if it wasn't going to make any difference.

He wasn't nearly as brisk now with his little black bag as he had been when he came in. He touched Mama's forehead a couple of times and it didn't feel good to him, I guess, because he looked tired after he did it. He held his hand on the wrist of her good arm, but I couldn't tell what this meant from his face. It mustn't have been any worse than the forehead, or maybe his face had nothing to do with what he thought, and I was imagining all this from seeing the shape Mama was in. Finally he said, "I'll try," and he began calling for hot water and other things, and pretty soon Mama was all bandaged up white.

The doctor stepped away from Mama and over to some men and women, six or seven of them now—a lot more had gone—and asked them what had happened. He didn't ask all the questions I wanted to ask—I guess he already knew some of the answers—but I did find out Mama was on a streetcar coming home from the plant—Mama works now and we're saving for a cranberry farm—when the riot broke out in that section. Mr. Purvine said he called the mill and told Daddy to come home. But Mr. Purvine said he wasn't going to work tonight himself, the way the riot was spreading and the way the coloreds were getting the worst of it.

"As usual," said a man with glasses on. "The Negroes ought to organize and fight the thing to a finish." The doctor frowned at that. Mr. Purvine said he didn't know. But one woman and another man said that was the right idea.

"If we must die," said the man with glasses on, "let it not be like hogs hunted and penned in an inglorious spot!"

The doctor said, "Yes, we all know that."

But the man with glasses on went on, because the others were listening to him, and I was glad he did, because I was listening to him too. "We must meet the common foe; though far outnumbered, let us still be brave, and for their thousand blows deal one deathblow! What, though before us lies the open grave? Like men we'll face the murderous, cowardly pack, pressed to the wall, dying, but—fighting back!"[1]

They all thought it was fine, and a woman said that it was poetry, and I thought if that is what it is I know what I want to be now—a poetryman. I asked the man with glasses on if that was his poetry, though I did not think it was for some reason, and the men and women all looked at me like they were surprised to see me there and like I ought not hear such things—except the man with glasses on, and he said, No, son, it was not his poetry; he wished it was, but it was Claude McKay's, a Negro, and I could find it in the public library. I decided I would go to the public library when the riot was over, and it was the first time in my life I ever thought of the public library the way I did then.

They all left about this time, except the doctor and the old woman friend of Old Gramma's. She came out of Old Gramma's room, and when the door opened I saw Old Gramma lying on the cot with her eyes closed. The old woman asked me if I could work a can opener, and I said, "Yes, I can," and she handed me a can of vegetable soup from the shelf. She got a meal together and us kids sat down to eat. Not Carrie, though. She sat in our good chair with her legs under her and her eyes closed. Mama was sleeping and the doctor rolled up the shade at the window and looked out while we ate. I mean brother George and the baby. I couldn't eat. I just drank my glass of water. The old woman said, Here, here, I hadn't ought to let good food go to waste and was that any way to act at the table and I wasn't the first boy in the world to lose his mother.

[1] From *Harlem Shadows*, by Claude McKay. Reprinted by permission of Harcourt, Brace and Company, Inc.

I wondered was she crazy and I yelled I wasn't going to lose my mother and I looked to see and I was right. Mama was just sleeping and the doctor was there in case she needed him and everything was taken care of and . . . everything. The doctor didn't even turn away from the window when I yelled at the old woman, and I thought at least he'd say I'd wake my mother up shouting that way, or maybe that I was right and the old woman was wrong. I got up from the table and stood by the doctor at the window. He only stayed there a minute more then and went over to feel Mama's wrist again. He did not touch her forehead this time.

Old Gramma came out of her room and said to me, "Was that you raising so much cain in here, boy?"

I said, "Yes, it was," and just when I was going to tell her what the old woman said about losing Mama I couldn't. I didn't want to hear it out loud again. I didn't even want to think it in my mind.

Old Gramma went over and gazed down at Mama. She turned away quickly and told the old woman, "Please, I'll just have a cup of hot water, that's all, I'm so upset." Then she went over to the doctor by the window and whispered something to him and he whispered something back and it must've been only one or two words, because he was looking out the window the next moment.

Old Gramma said she'd be back in a minute and went out the door, slipslapping down the hall. I went to the window, the evening sun was going down, and I saw Old Gramma come out the back entrance of our building. She crossed the alley and went in the back door of the grocery store.

A lot of racket cut loose about a block up the alley. It was still empty, though. Old Gramma came out of the grocery store with something in a brown bag. She stopped in the middle of the alley and seemed to be watching the orange evening sun going down behind the buildings. The sun got in her hair and somehow under her skin, kind of, and it did a wonderful thing to her. She looked so young for a moment that I saw Mama in her, both of them beautiful New Orleans ladies.

The racket cut loose again, nearer now, and a pack of

men came running down the alley, about three dozen whites chasing two coloreds. One of the whites was blowing a bugle—*tan tivvy, tan tivvy, tan tivvy*—like the white folks do when they go fox hunting in the movies or Virginia. I looked down, quick, to see if Old Gramma had enough sense to come inside, and I guess she did because she wasn't there. The two coloreds ran between two buildings, the whites ran after them, and then the alley was quiet again. Old Gramma stepped out, and I watched her stoop and pick up the brown bag that she had dropped before.

Another big noise made her drop it again. A whole smear of men swarmed out of the used-car lot and came galloping down the alley like wild buffaloes. Old Gramma scooted inside our building and the brown bag stayed there in the alley. This time I couldn't believe my eyes; I saw what I thought I'd never see; I saw what us kids had been waiting to see ever since the riot broke out—a white man that was fixing to get himself nice and killed. A white man running —running, God Almighty, from about a million coloreds. And he was the one with the tan-tivvy bugle, too. I hoped the coloreds would do the job up right.

The closer the white man came the worse it got for him, because the alley comes to a dead end when it hits our building. All at once—I don't know why—I was praying for that fool white man with the bugle to get away. But I didn't think he had a Chinaman's chance, the way he was going now, and maybe that's what made me pray for him.

Then he did a smart thing. He whipped the bugle over his shoulder, like you do with a horseshoe for good luck, and it hit the first colored behind him smack in the head, knocking him out, and that slowed up the others. The white man turned into the junk yard behind the furniture warehouse and the Victory Ballroom. Another smart thing, if he used his head. The space between the warehouse and the Victory is just wide enough for a man to run through. It's a long piece to the street, but if he made it there, he'd be safe probably.

The long passageway must've looked too narrow to him, though, because the fool came rushing around the garage next to our building. For a moment he was the only one in the alley. The coloreds had followed him through the junk yard and probably got themselves all tangled up in garbage cans and rusty bed springs and ashpiles. But the white man was a goner just the same. In a minute they'd be coming for him for real. He'd have to run the length of the alley again to get away and the coloreds have got the best legs.

Then Old Gramma opened our back door and saved him.

I was very glad for the white man, until suddenly I remembered poor Mama all broken to pieces on the bed, and then I was sorry Old Gramma did it. The next moment I was glad again that she did. I understood now I did not care one way or the other about the white man. Now I was thinking of Mama—not of myself. I did not see what difference it could make to Mama if the white man lived or died. It only had something to do with us and him.

Then I got hold of a funny idea. I told myself the trouble is somebody gets cheated or insulted or killed and everybody else tries to make it come out even by cheating and insulting and killing the cheaters and insulters and killers. Only they never do. I did not think they ever would. I told myself that I had a very big idea there, and when the riot was over I would go to the public library and sit in the reading room and think about it. Or I would speak to Old Gramma about it, because it seemed like she had the same big idea and like she had had it a long time, too.

The doctor was standing by me at the window all the time. He said nothing about what Old Gramma did, and now he stepped away from the window and so did I. I guess he felt the same way I did about the white man and that's why he stepped away from the window. The big idea again. He was afraid the coloreds down below would yell up at us, did we see the white man pass by. The coloreds were crazy mad all right. One of them had the white man's bugle and he banged on our door with it. I was worried Old Gramma had forgot to lock it and they might walk right in, and that would be the end of the white man and the big idea.

But Old Gramma pulled another fast one. She ran out into the alley and pointed her old yellow finger in about three wrong directions. In a second the alley was quiet and empty, except for Old Gramma. She walked slowly over

against our building, where somebody had kicked the
brown bag, and picked it up.

Old Gramma brought the white man right into our room,
told him to sit down, and poured herself a cup of hot water.
She sipped it and said the white man could leave whenever
he wanted to, but it might be better to wait a bit. The
white man said he was much obliged, he hated to give us
any trouble, and, "Oh, oh, is somebody sick over there?"
when he saw Mama, and that he'd just been passing by
when a hundred nig—when he was attacked.

Old Gramma sipped her hot water. The doctor turned
away from the window and said, "Here they come again,"
took another look, and said, "No, they're going back." He
went over to Mama and held her wrist. I couldn't tell anything about her from his face. She was sleeping just the
same. The doctor asked the white man, still standing, to sit
down. Carrie only opened her eyes once and closed them.
She hadn't changed her position in the good chair. Brother
George and the baby stood in a corner with their eyes on
the white man. The baby's legs buckled then—she'd only
been walking about a week—and she collapsed softly to the
floor. She worked her way up again without taking her eyes
off the white man. He even looked funny and out of place
to me in our room. I guess the man for the rent and Father
Egan were the only white people come to see us since I
could remember; and now it was only the man for the rent
since Father Egan died.

The doctor asked the white man did he work or own a
business in this neighborhood. The white man said, No,
glancing down at his feet, no, he just happened to be passing by when he was suddenly attacked like he said before.
The doctor told Old Gramma she might wash Mama's face
and neck again with warm water.

There was noise again in the alley—windows breaking and
fences being pushed over. The doctor said to the white
man, "You could leave now; it's a white mob this time;
you'd be safe."

"No," the white man said, "I should say not; I wouldn't
be seen with them; they're as bad as the others almost."

"It is quite possible," the doctor said.

Old Gramma asked the white man if he would like a cup of tea.

"Tea? No," he said, "I don't drink tea; I didn't know you drank it."

"I didn't know you knew her," the doctor said, looking at Old Gramma and the white man.

"You colored folks, I mean," the white man said, "Americans, I mean. Me, I don't drink tea—always considered it an English drink and bad for the kidneys."

The doctor did not answer. Old Gramma brought him a cup of tea.

And then Daddy came in. He ran over to Mama and fell down on his knees like he was dead—like seeing Mama with her arm broke and her chest so pushed in killed him on the spot. He lifted his face from the bed and kissed Mama on the lips; and then, Daddy, I could see, was crying—the strongest man in the world was crying with tears in his big dark eyes and coming down the side of his big hard face. Mama called him her John Henry sometimes and there he was, her John Henry, the strongest man, black or white, in the whole damn world, crying.

He put his head down on the bed again. Nobody in the room moved until the baby toddled over to Daddy and patted him on the ear like she wanted to play the games those two make up with her little hands and his big ears and eyes and nose. But Daddy didn't move or say anything, if he even knew she was there, and the baby got a blank look in her eyes and walked away from Daddy and sat down, *plump*, on the floor across the room, staring at Daddy and the white man, back and forth, Daddy and the white man.

Daddy got up after a while and walked very slowly across the room and got himself a drink of water at the sink. For the first time he noticed the white man in the room. "Who's he?" he said. "Who's he?" None of us said anything. "Who the hell's he?" Daddy wanted to know, thunder in his throat like there always is when he's extra mad or happy.

The doctor said the white man was Mr. Gorman, and went over to Daddy and told him something in a low voice.

"Innocent! What's he doing in this neighborhood then?" Daddy said, loud as before. "What's an *innocent* white man doing in this neighborhood now? Answer me that!" He looked at all of us in the room and none of us that knew what the white man was doing in this neighborhood wanted to explain to Daddy. Old Gramma and the doctor and me —none of us that knew—would tell.

"I was just passing by," the white man said, "as they can tell you."

The scared way he said it almost made me laugh. Was this a white *man*, I asked myself. Alongside Daddy's voice the white man's sounded plain foolish and weak—a little old tug squeaking at a big ocean liner about the right of way. Daddy seemed to forget all about him and began asking the doctor a lot of questions about Mama in a hoarse whisper I couldn't hear very well. Daddy's face got harder and harder and it didn't look like he'd ever crack a smile or shed a tear or anything soft again. Just hard, it got, hard as four spikes.

Old Gramma came and stood by Daddy's side and said she had called the priest when she was downstairs a while ago getting some candles. She was worried that the candles weren't blessed ones. She opened the brown bag then, and that's what was inside—two white candles. I didn't know grocery stores carried them.

Old Gramma went to her room and took down the picture of the Sacred Heart all bleeding and put it on the little table by Mama's bed and set the candles in sticks on each side of it. She lit the candles and it made the Sacred Heart, punctured by the wreath of thorns, look bloodier than ever, and made me think of that song, "To Jesus' Heart All Burning," the kids sing at Our Saviour's on Sundays.

The white man went up to the doctor and said, "I'm a Catholic, too." But the doctor didn't say anything back, only nodded. He probably wasn't one himself, I thought; not many of the race are. Our family wouldn't be if Old Gramma and Mama didn't come from New Orleans, where Catholics are thicker than flies or Baptists.

Daddy got up from the table and said to the white man, "So help me God, mister, I'll kill you in this room if my wife dies!" The baby started crying and the doctor went to

Daddy's side and turned him away from the white man, and it wasn't hard to do because now Daddy was kind of limp and didn't look like he remembered anything about the white man or what he said he'd do to him if Mama . . . or anything.

"I'll bet the priest won't show up," Daddy said.

"The priest will come," Old Gramma said. "The priest will always come when you need him; just wait." Her old lips were praying in French.

I hoped he would come like Old Gramma said, but I wasn't so sure. Some of the priests weren't much different from anybody else. They knew how to keep their necks in. Daddy said to Mama once if you only wanted to hear about social justice you could turn on the radio or go to the nearest stadium on the Fourth of July, and there'd be an old white man in a new black suit saying it was a good thing and everybody ought to get some, and if they'd just kick in more they might and, anyway, they'd be saved. One came to Our Saviour's last year, and Father Egan said this is our new assistant and the next Sunday our new assistant was gone—poor health. But Daddy said he was transferred to a church in a white neighborhood because he couldn't stand to save black souls. Father Egan would've come a-flying, riot or no riot, but he was dead now and we didn't know much about the one that took his place.

Then he came, by God; the priest from Our Saviour's came to our room while the riot was going on. Old Gramma got all excited and said over and over she knew the priest would come. He was kind of young and skinny and pale, even for a white man, and he said, "I'm Father Crowe," to everybody in the room and looked around to see who was who.

The doctor introduced himself and said Old Gramma was Old Gramma, Daddy was Daddy, we were the children, that was Mr. Gorman, who was just passing by, and over there was poor Mama. He missed Old Gramma's old woman friend; I guess he didn't know what to call her. The priest went over and took a look at Mama and nodded to the doctor and they went into Old Gramma's room together. The priest had a little black bag, too, and he took it with him.

I suppose he was getting ready to give Mama Extreme Unction. I didn't think they would wake her up for Confession or Holy Communion; she was so weak and needed the rest.

Daddy got up from the table mad as a bull and said to the white man, "Remember what I said, mister."

"But why me?" the white man asked. "Just because I'm white?"

Daddy looked over at Mama on the bed and said, "Yeah, just because you're white; yeah, that's why. . . ." Old Gramma took Daddy by the arm and steered him over to the table again and he sat down.

The priest and the doctor came out of Old Gramma's room, and right away the priest faced the white man, like they'd been talking about him in Old Gramma's room, and asked him why he didn't go home. The white man said he'd heard some shouting in the alley a while ago that didn't sound so good to him and he didn't think it was safe yet and that was why.

"I see," the priest said.

"I'm a Catholic too, Father," the white man said.

"That's the trouble," the priest said.

The priest took some cotton from his little black bag, dipped his fingers in holy oil, and made the sign of the cross on Mama's eyes, nose, ears, mouth, and hands, rubbing the oil off with the cotton, and said prayers in Latin all the time he was doing it.

"I want you all to kneel down now," the priest said, "and we'll say a rosary. But we mustn't say it too loud because she is sleeping."

We all knelt down except the baby and Carrie. Carrie said she'd never kneel down to God again. "Now Carrie," Old Gramma said, almost crying. She told Carrie it was for poor Mama and wouldn't Carrie kneel down if it was for poor Mama?

"No!" Carrie said. "It must be a white God too!" Then she began crying and she did kneel down after all.

Even the white man knelt down and the doctor and the old woman friend of Old Gramma's, a solid Baptist if I ever saw one, and we all said the rosary of the five sorrowful mysteries.

Afterwards the white man said to the priest, "Do you mind if I leave when you do, Father?" The priest didn't answer, and the white man said, "I think I'll be leaving now, Father. I wonder if you'd be going my way?"

The priest finally said, "All right, all right, come along. You won't be the first one to hide behind a Roman collar."

The white man said, "I'm sure I don't know what you mean by that, Father." The priest didn't hear him, I guess, or want to explain, because he went over to Mama's bed.

The priest knelt once more by Mama and said a prayer in Latin out loud and made the sign of the cross over Mama: *In nomine Patris et Filii et Spiritus Sancti.* He looked closer at Mama and motioned to the doctor. The doctor stepped over to the bed, felt Mama's wrist, put his head to her chest, where it wasn't pushed in, and stood up slowly.

Daddy and all of us had been watching the doctor when the priest motioned him over, and now Daddy got up from the table, kicking the chair over he got up so fast, and ran to the bed. Shaking all over, he sank to his knees, and I believe he must've been crying again, although I thought he never would again and his head was down and I couldn't see for sure.

I began to get an awful bulging pain in my stomach. The doctor left the bed and grabbed the white man by the arm and was taking him to the door when Daddy jumped up, like he knew where they were going, and said, "Wait a minute, mister!"

The doctor and the white man stopped at the door. Daddy walked draggily over to them and stood in front of the white man, took a deep breath, and said in the stillest kind of whisper, "I wouldn't touch you." That was all. He moved slowly back to Mama's bed and his big shoulders were sagged down like I never saw them before.

Old Gramma said, "*Jésus!*" and stumbled down on her knees by Mama. Then the awful bulging pain in my stomach exploded, and I knew that Mama wasn't just sleeping now, and I couldn't breathe for a long while, and then when I finally could I was crying like the baby and brother George, and so was Carrie.

Lions, Harts, Leaping Does

" 'Thirty-ninth pope. Anastasius, a Roman, appointed that while the Gospel was reading they should stand and not sit. He exempted from the ministry those that were lame, impotent, or diseased persons, and slept with his forefathers in peace, being a confessor.' "

"Anno?"

" 'Anno 404.' "

They sat there in the late afternoon, the two old men grown gray in the brown robes of the Order. Angular winter daylight forsook the small room, almost a cell in the primitive sense, and passed through the window into the outside world. The distant horizon, which it sought to join, was still bright and strong against approaching night. The old Franciscans, one priest, one brother, were left among the shadows in the room.

"Can you see to read one more, Titus?" the priest Didymus asked. "Number fourteen." He did not cease staring out the window at day becoming night on the horizon. The thirty-ninth pope said Titus might not be a priest. Did Titus, reading, understand? He could never really tell about Titus, who said nothing now. There was only silence, then a dry whispering of pages turning. "Number fourteen," Didymus said. "That's Zephyrinus. I always like the old heretic on that one, Titus."

According to one bibliographer, Bishop Bale's *Pageant of Popes Contayninge the Lyves of all the Bishops of Rome, from the Beginninge of them to the Year of Grace 1555* was a denunciation of every pope from Peter to Paul IV. However inviting to readers that might sound, it was in sober fact a lie. The first popes, persecuted and mostly martyred, wholly escaped the author's remarkable spleen and even enjoyed his crusty approbation. Father Didymus, his aged appetite for biography jaded by the orthodox lives, found the work fascinating. He usually referred to it as "Bishop Bale's funny book" and to the Bishop as a heretic.

Titus squinted at the yellowed page. He snapped a glance at the light hovering at the window. Then he closed his eyes and with great feeling recited:

"'O how joyous and how delectable is it to see religious men devout and fervent in the love of God, well-mannered—'"

"Titus," Didymus interrupted softly.

"'—and well taught in ghostly learning.'"

"Titus, read." Didymus placed the words in their context. The First Book of *The Imitation* and Chapter, if he was not mistaken, XXV. The trick was no longer in finding the source of Titus's quotations; it was putting them in their exact context. It had become an unconfessed contest between them, and it gratified Didymus to think he had been able to place the fragment. Titus knew two books by heart, *The Imitation* and *The Little Flowers of St. Francis*. Lately, unfortunately, he had begun to learn another. He was more and more quoting from Bishop Bale. Didymus reminded himself he must not let Titus read past the point where the martyred popes left off. What Bale had to say about Peter's later successors sounded incongruous—"unmete" in the old heretic's own phrase—coming from a Franciscan brother. Two fathers had already inquired of Didymus concerning Titus. One had noted the antique style of his words and had ventured to wonder if Brother Titus, Christ preserve us, might be slightly possessed. He cited the case of the illiterate Missouri farmer who cursed the Church in a forgotten Aramaic tongue.

"Read, Titus."

Titus squinted at the page once more and read in his fine dead voice.

"'Fourteenth pope, Zephyrinus. Zephyrinus was a Roman born, a man as writers do testify, more addicted with all endeavor to the service of God than to the cure of any worldly affairs. Whereas before his time the wine in the celebrating the communion was ministered in a cup of wood, he first did alter that, and instead thereof brought in cups or chalices of glass. And yet he did not this upon any superstition, as thinking wood to be unlawful, or glass to be more holy for that use, but because the one is more comely and seemly, as by experience it appeareth than the other. And yet some wooden dolts do dream that the wooden cups were changed by him because that part of the wine, or as they thought, the royal blood of Christ, did soak into the wood, and so it can not be in glass. Surely sooner may wine soak into any wood than any wit into those winey heads that thus both deceive themselves and slander this Godly martyr.' "

"Anno?"

Titus squinted at the page again. " 'Anno 222,' " he read.

They were quiet for a moment which ended with the clock in the tower booming once for the half hour. Didymus got up and stood so close to the window his breath became visible. Noticing it, he inhaled deeply and then, exhaling, he sent a gust of smoke churning against the freezing pane, clouding it. Some old unmelted snow in tree crotches lay dirty and white in the gathering dark.

"It's cold out today," Didymus said.

He stepped away from the window and over to Titus, whose face was relaxed in open-eyed sleep. He took Bishop Bale's funny book unnoticed from Titus's hands.

"Thank you, Titus," he said.

Titus blinked his eyes slowly once, then several times quickly. His body gave a shudder, as if coming to life.

"Yes, Father?" he was asking.

"I said thanks for reading. You are a great friend to me."

"Yes, Father."

"I know you'd rather read other authors." Didymus moved to the window, stood there gazing through the tops of trees, their limbs black and bleak against the sky. He rubbed his hands. "I'm going for a walk before vespers. Is it too cold for you, Titus?"

" 'A good religious man that is fervent in his religion taketh all things well, and doth gladly all that he is commanded to do.' "

Didymus, walking across the room, stopped and looked at Titus just in time to see him open his eyes. He was quoting again: *The Imitation* and still in Chapter XXV. Why had he said that? To himself Didymus repeated the words and decided Titus, his mind moving intelligently but

so pathetically largo, was documenting the act of reading
Bishop Bale when there were other books he preferred.

"I'm going out for a walk," Didymus said.

Titus rose and pulled down the full sleeves of his brown
robe in anticipation of the cold.

"I think it is too cold for you, Titus," Didymus said.

Titus faced him undaunted, arms folded and hands
muffled in his sleeves, eyes twinkling incredulously. He was
ready to go. Didymus got the idea Titus knew himself to
be the healthier of the two. Didymus was vaguely annoyed
at this manifestation of the truth. *Vanitas.*

"Won't they need you in the kitchen now?" he inquired.

Immediately he regretted having said that. And the way
he had said it, with some malice, as though labor *per se*
were important and the intention not so. *Vanitas* in a friar,
and at his age too. Confronting Titus with a distinction his
simple mind could never master and which, if it could, his
great soul would never recognize. Titus only knew all that
was necessary, that a friar did what he was best at in the
community. And no matter the nature of his toil, the
variety of the means at hand, the end was the same for all
friars. Or indeed for all men, if they cared to know. Titus
worked in the kitchen and garden. Was Didymus wrong
in teaching geometry out of personal preference and perhaps—if this was so he was—out of pride? Had the spiritual
worth of his labor been vitiated because of that? He did
not think so, no. No, he taught geometry because it was
useful and eternally true, like his theology, and though of a
lower order of truth it escaped the common fate of theology
and the humanities, perverted through the ages in the
mouths of dunderheads and fools. From that point of view,
his work came to the same thing as Titus's. The vineyard
was everywhere; they were in it, and that was essential.

Didymus, consciously humble, held open the door for
Titus. Sandals scraping familiarly, they passed through
dark corridors until they came to the stairway. Lights from
floors above and below spangled through the carven aper-
tures of the winding stair and fell in confusion upon the
worn oaken steps.

At the outside door they were ambushed. An old friar

stepped out of the shadows to intercept them. Standing with Didymus and Titus, however, made him appear younger. Or possibly it was the tenseness of him.

"Good evening, Father," he said to Didymus. "And Titus."

Didymus nodded in salutation and Titus said deliberately, as though he were the first one ever to put words in such conjunction:

"Good evening, Father Rector."

The Rector watched Didymus expectantly. Didymus studied the man's face. It told him nothing but curiosity—a luxury which could verge on vice in the cloister. Didymus frowned his incomprehension. He was about to speak. He decided against it, turning to Titus:

"Come on, Titus, we've got a walk to take before vespers."

The Rector was left standing.

They began to circle the monastery grounds. Away from the buildings it was brighter. With a sudden shudder, Didymus felt the freezing air bite into his body all over. Instinctively he drew up his cowl. That was a little better. Not much. It was too cold for him to relax, breathe deeply, and stride freely. It had not looked this cold from his window. He fell into Titus's gait. The steps were longer, but there was an illusion of warmth about moving in unison. Bit by bit he found himself duplicating every aspect of Titus in motion. Heads down, eyes just ahead of the next step, undeviating, they seemed peripatetic figures in a Gothic frieze. The stones of the walk were trampled over with frozen footsteps. Titus's feet were gray and bare in their open sandals. Pieces of ice, the thin edges of ruts, cracked off under foot, skittering sharply away. A crystal fragment lit between Titus's toes and did not melt there. He did not seem to notice it. This made Didymus lift his eyes.

A fine Franciscan! Didymus snorted, causing a flurry of vapors. He had the despicable caution of the comfortable who move mountains, if need be, to stay that way. Here he was, cowl up and heavy woolen socks on, and regretting the weather because it exceeded his anticipations. Painfully he stubbed his toe on purpose and at once accused himself of exhibitionism. Then he damned the expression for its modernity. He asked himself wherein lay the renunciation of the world, the flesh and the devil, the whole point of following after St. Francis today. Poverty, Chastity, Obedience—the three vows. There was nothing of suffering in the poverty of the friar nowadays: he was penniless, but materially rich compared to—what was the phrase he used to hear?—"one third of the nation." A beggar, a homeless mendicant by very definition, he knew nothing—except as it affected others "less fortunate"—of the miseries of begging in the streets. Verily, it was no heavy cross, this vow of Poverty, so construed and practiced, in the modern world. Begging had become unfashionable. Somewhere along the line the meaning had been lost; they had become too "fortunate." Official agencies, to whom it was a nasty but necessary business, dispensed Charity without mercy or grace. He recalled with wry amusement Frederick Barbarossa's appeal to fellow princes when opposed by the might of the medieval Church: "We have a clean conscience, and it tells us that God is with us. Ever have we striven to bring back priests and, in especial, those of the topmost rank, to the condition of the first Christian Church. In those days the clergy raised their eyes to the angels, shone through miracles, made whole the sick, raised the dead, made Kings and Princes subject to them, not with arms but with their holiness. But now they are smothered in delights. To withdraw from them the harmful riches which burden them to their own undoing is a labor of love in which all Princes should eagerly participate."

And Chastity, what of that? Well, that was all over for him—a battle he had fought and won many years ago. A sin whose temptations had prevailed undiminished through the centuries, but withal for him, an old man, a dead issue, a young man's trial. Only Obedience remained, and that, too, was no longer difficult for him. There was something —much as he disliked the term—to be said for "conditioning." He had to smile at himself: why should he bristle so at using the word? It was only contemporary slang for a theory the Church had always known. "Psychiatry," so called, and all the ghastly superstition that attended its practice, the deification of its high priests in the secular schools, made him ill. But it would pass. Just look how alchemy had flourished, and where was it today?

Clearly an abecedarian observance of the vows did not promise perfection. Stemmed in divine wisdom, they were branches meant to flower forth, but requiring of the friar the water and sunlight of sacrifice. The letter led nowhere. It was the spirit of the vows which opened the way and revealed to the soul, no matter the flux of circumstance, the means of salvation.

He had picked his way through the welter of familiar factors again—again to the same bitter conclusion. He had come to the key and core of his trouble anew. When he received the letter from Seraphin asking him to come to St. Louis, saying his years prohibited unnecessary travel and endowed his request with a certain prerogative—No, he had written back, it's simply impossible, not saying why. God help him, as a natural man, he had the desire, perhaps the inordinate desire, to see his brother again. He should not have to prove that. One of them must die soon. But as a friar, he remembered: "Unless a man be clearly delivered from the love of all creatures, he may not fully tend to his Creator." Therein, he thought, the keeping of the vows having become an easy habit for him, was his opportunity—he thought! It was plain and there was sacrifice and it would be hard. So he had not gone.

Now it was plain that he had been all wrong. Seraphin was an old man with little left to warm him in the world. Didymus asked himself—recoiling at the answer before the question was out—if his had been the only sacrifice. Rather, had he not been too intent on denying himself at the time to notice that he was denying Seraphin also? Harshly Didymus told himself he had used his brother for a hair shirt. This must be the truth, he thought; it hurts so.

The flesh just above his knees felt frozen. They were drawing near the entrance again. His face, too, felt the same way, like a slab of pasteboard, stiffest at the tip of his nose. When he wrinkled his brow and puffed out his cheeks to blow hot air up to his nose, his skin seemed to crackle

like old parchment. His eyes watered from the wind. He
pressed a hand, warm from his sleeve, to his exposed
neck. Frozen, like his face. It would be chapped tomorrow.

Titus, white hair awry in the wind, looked just the same.

They entered the monastery door. The Rector stopped
them. It was almost as before, except that Didymus was
occupied with feeling his face and patting it back to life.

"Ah, Didymus! It must be cold indeed!" The Rector
smiled at Titus and returned his gaze to Didymus. He
made it appear that they were allied in being amused at
Didymus's face. Didymus touched his nose tenderly. Assured it would stand the operation, he blew it lustily. He
stuffed the handkerchief up his sleeve. The Rector, misin-
terpreting all this ceremony, obviously was afraid of being
ignored.

"The telegram, Didymus. I'm sorry; I thought it might
have been important."

"I received no telegram."

They faced each other, waiting, experiencing a hanging
moment of uneasiness.

Then, having employed the deductive method, they
both looked at Titus. Although he had not been listening,
rather had been studying the naked toes in his sandals, he
sensed their eyes questioning him.

"Yes, Father Rector?" he answered.

"The telegram for Father Didymus, Titus?" the Rector
demanded. "Where is it?" Titus started momentarily out
of willingness to be of service, but ended, his mind refusing
to click, impassive before them. The Rector shook his head
in faint exasperation and reached his hand down into the
folds of Titus's cowl. He brought forth two envelopes. One,
the telegram, he gave to Didymus. The other, a letter, he
handed back to Titus.

"I gave you this letter this morning, Titus. It's for Father
Anthony." Intently Titus stared unremembering at the
letter. "I wish you would see that Father Anthony gets it
right away, Titus. I think it's a bill."

Titus held the envelope tightly to his breast and said,
"Father Anthony."

Then his eyes were attracted by the sound of Didymus

tearing open the telegram. While Didymus read the telegram, Titus's expression showed he at last understood his failure to deliver it. He was perturbed, mounting inner distress moving his lips silently.

Didymus looked up from the telegram. He saw the grief in Titus's face and said, astonished, "How did you know, Titus?"

Titus's eyes were both fixed and lowered in sorrow. It seemed to Didymus that Titus knew the meaning of the telegram. Didymus was suddenly weak, as before a miracle. His eyes went to the Rector to see how he was taking it. Then it occurred to him the Rector could not know what had happened.

As though nothing much had, the Rector laid an absolving hand lightly upon Titus's shoulder.

"Didymus, he can't forgive himself for not delivering the telegram now that he remembers it. That's all."

Didymus was relieved. Seeing the telegram in his hand, he folded it quickly and stuffed it back in the envelope. He handed it to the Rector. calmly, in a voice quite drained of feeling, he said, "My brother, Father Seraphin, died last night in St. Louis."

"Father Seraphin *from Rome?*"

"Yes," Didymus said, "in St. Louis. He was my brother. Appointed a confessor in Rome, a privilege for a foreigner. He was ninety-two."

"I know that, Didymus, an honor for the Order. I had no idea he was in this country. Ninety-two! God rest his soul!"

"I had a letter from him only recently."

"You did?"

"He wanted me to come to St. Louis. I hadn't seen him for twenty-five years at least."

"Twenty-five years?"

"It was impossible for me to visit him."

"But if he was in this country, Didymus . . ."

The Rector waited for Didymus to explain.

Didymus opened his mouth to speak, heard the clock in the tower sound the quarter hour, and said nothing, listening, lips parted, to the last of the strokes die away.

"Why, Didymus, it could easily have been arranged," the Rector persisted.

Didymus turned abruptly to Titus, who, standing in a dream, had been inattentive since the clock struck.

"Come, Titus, we'll be late."

He hastened down the corridor with Titus. "No," he said in agitation, causing Titus to look at him in surprise. "I told him no. It was simply impossible." He was conscious of Titus's attention. "To visit him, Seraphin, who is dead." That had come naturally enough, for being the first time in his thoughts that Seraphin was dead. Was there not some merit in his dispassionate acceptance of the fact?

They entered the chapel for vespers and knelt down.

The clock struck. One, two . . . two. Two? No, there must have been one or two strokes before. He had gone to sleep. It was three. At least three, probably four. Or five. He waited. It could not be two: he remembered the brothers filing darkly into the chapel at that hour. Disturbing the shadows for matins and lauds. If it was five—he listened for faint noises in the building—it would only be a few minutes. They would come in, the earliest birds, to say their Masses. There were no noises. He looked toward the windows on the St. Joseph side of the chapel. He might be able to see a light from a room across the court. That was not certain even if it was five. It would have to come through the stained glass. Was that possible? It was still night. Was there a moon? He looked round the chapel. If there was, it might shine on a window. There was no moon. Or it was overhead. Or powerless against the glass. He yawned. It could not be five. His knees were numb from kneeling. He shifted on them. His back ached. Straightening it, he gasped for breath. He saw the sanctuary light. The only light, red. Then it came back to him. Seraphin was dead. He tried to pray. No words. Why words? Meditation in the Presence. The perfect prayer. He fell asleep . . .

. . . Spiraling brown coil on coil under the golden sun the river slithered across the blue and flower-flecked land. On an eminence they held identical hands over their eyes for visors and mistook it with pleasure for an endless mur-

muring serpent. They considered unafraid the prospect of
its turning in its course and standing on tail to swallow
them gurgling alive. They sensed it was in them to com-
mand this also by a wish. Their visor hands vanished before
their eyes and became instead the symbol of brotherhood
clasped between them. This they wished. Smiling the same
smile back and forth they began laughing: "Jonah!" And
were walking murkily up and down the brown belly of the
river in mock distress. Above them, foolishly triumphant,
rippling in contentment, mewed the waves. Below swam an
occasional large fish, absorbed in ignoring them, and the
mass of crustacea, eagerly seething, too numerous on the
bottom to pretend exclusiveness. "Jonah indeed!" the brothers said, surprised to see the bubbles they birthed. They
strolled then for hours this way. The novelty wearing off
(without regret, else they would have wished themselves
elsewhere), they began to talk and say ordinary things.
Their mother had died, their father too, and how old did
that make them? It was the afternoon of the funerals, which
they had managed, transcending time, to have held jointly.
She had seemed older and for some reason he otherwise.
How, they wondered, should it be with them, *memento
mori* clicking simultaneously within them, lackaday. The
sound of dirt descending six feet to clatter on the coffins
was memorable but unmentionable. Their own lives, well
. . . only half curious (something to do) they halted to
kick testily a waterlogged rowboat resting on the bottom,
the crustacea complaining and olive-green silt rising to
speckle the surface with dark stars . . . well, what *had*
they been doing? A crayfish pursued them, clad in sable
armor, dearly desiring to do battle, brandishing hinged
swords. Well, for one thing, working for the canonization
of Fra Bartolomeo, had got two cardinals interested, was
hot after those remaining who were at all possible, a slow
business. Yes, one would judge so in the light of past can-
onizations, though being stationed in Rome had its advan-
tages. Me, the same old grind, teaching, pounding away,
giving Pythagoras no rest in his grave . . . They made an
irresolute pass at the crayfish, who had caught up with
them. More about Fra Bartolomeo, what else is there? Ex-

cept, you will laugh or have me excommunicated for wanton presumption, though it's only faith in a faithless age, making a vow not to die until he's made a saint, recognized rather—he is one, convinced of it, Didymus (never can get used to calling you that), a saint sure as I'm alive, having known him, no doubt of it, something wrong with your knee? Knees then! The crayfish, he's got hold of you there, another at your back. If you like, we'll leave—only I do like it here. Well, go ahead then, you never did like St. Louis, isn't that what you used to say? Alone, in pain, he rose to the surface, parting the silt stars. The sun like molten gold squirted him in the eye. Numb now, unable to remember, and too blind to refurnish his memory by observation, he waited for this limbo to clear away. . . .

Awake now, he was face to face with a flame, blinding him. He avoided it. A dead weight bore him down, his aching back. Slowly, like ink in a blotter, his consciousness spread. The supports beneath him were kneeling limbs, his, the veined hands, bracing him, pressing flat, his own. His body, it seemed, left off there; the rest was something else, floor. He raised his head to the flame again and tried to determine what kept it suspended even with his face. He shook his head, blinking dumbly, a four-legged beast. He could see nothing, only his knees and hands, which he felt rather, and the flame floating unaccountably in the darkness. That part alone was a mystery. And then there came a pressure and pull on his shoulders, urging him up. Fingers, a hand, a rustling related to its action, then the rustling in rhythm with the folds of a brown curtain, a robe naturally, ergo a friar, holding a candle, trying to raise him up, Titus. The clock began striking.

"Put out the candle," Didymus said.

Titus closed his palm slowly around the flame, unflinching, snuffing it. The odor of burning string. Titus pinched the wick deliberately. He waited a moment, the clock falling silent, and said, "Father Rector expects you will say a Mass for the Dead at five o'clock."

"Yes, I know." He yawned deliciously. "I told him *that*." He bit his lips at the memory of the disgusting yawn. Titus had found him asleep. Shame overwhelmed him, and he searched his mind for justification. He found none.

"It is five now," Titus said.

It was maddening. "I don't see anyone else if it's five," he snapped. Immediately he was aware of a light burning in the sacristy. He blushed and grew pale. Had someone besides Titus seen him sleeping? But, listening, he heard nothing. No one else was up yet. He was no longer pale and was only blushing now. He saw it all hopefully. He was saved. Titus had gone to the sacristy to prepare for Mass. He must have come out to light the candles on the main altar. Then he had seen the bereaved keeping vigil on all fours, asleep, snoring even. What did Titus think of that? It withered him to remember, but he was comforted some that the only witness had been Titus. Had the sleeping apostles in Gethsemane been glad it was Christ?

Wrong! Hopelessly wrong! For there had come a noise after all. Someone else was in the sacristy. He stiffened and walked palely toward it. He must go there and get ready to say his Mass. A few steps he took only, his back buckling out, humping, his knees sinking to the floor, his hands last. The floor, with fingers smelling of dust and genesis, reached up and held him. The fingers were really spikes and they were dusty from holding him this way all his life. For a radiant instant, which had something of eternity about it, he saw the justice of his position. Then there was nothing.

A little snow had fallen in the night, enough to powder the dead grass and soften the impression the leafless trees etched in the sky. Grayly the sky promised more snow, but now, at the end of the day following his collapse in the chapel, it was melting. Didymus, bundled around by blankets, sat in a wheel chair at the window, unsleepy. Only the landscape wearied him. Dead and unmoving though it must be—of that he was sure—it conspired to make him see everything in it as living, moving, something to be watched, each visible tuft of grass, each cluster of snow. The influence of the snow perhaps? For the ground, ordinarily uniform in texture and drabness, had split up into individual patches. They appeared to be involved in a struggle of some kind, possibly to overlap each other, constantly shifting. But whether it was equally one against one, or one against all, he could not make out. He reminded himself he did not believe it was actually happening. It was confusing and he closed his eyes. After a time this confused and tired him in the same way. The background of darkness became a field of varicolored factions, warring, and, worse than the landscape, things like worms and comets wriggled and exploded before his closed eyes. Finally, as though to orchestrate their motions, they carried with them a bewildering noise or music which grew louder and cacophonous. The effect was cumulative, inevitably unbearable, and Didymus would have to open his eyes again. The intervals of peace became gradually rarer on the landscape. Likewise when he shut his eyes to it the restful darkness dissolved sooner than before into riot.

The door of his room opened, mercifully dispelling his illusions, and that, because there had been no knock, could only be Titus. Unable to move in his chair, Didymus listened to Titus moving about the room at his back. The tinkle of a glass once, the squeak of the bookcase indicating a book taken out or replaced—they were sounds Didymus could recognize. But that first tap-tap and the consequent click of metal on metal, irregular and scarcely audible, was disconcertingly unfamiliar. His curiosity, centering on it, raised it to a delicious mystery. He kept down the urge to shout at Titus. But he attempted to fish from memory the precise character of the corner from which the sound came with harrowing repetition. The sound stopped then, as though to thwart him on the brink of revelation. Titus's footsteps scraped across the room. The door opened and closed. For a few steps, Didymus heard Titus going down the corridor. He asked himself not to be moved by idle curiosity, a thing of the senses. He would not be tempted now.

A moment later the keystone of his good intention crumbled, and the whole edifice of his detachment with it. More shakily than quickly, Didymus moved his hands to the wheels of the chair. He would roll over to the corner and investigate the sound. . . . He would? His hands lay limply on the wheels, ready to propel him to his mind's destination, but, weak, white, powerless to grip the wheels or anything. He regarded them with contempt. He had known they would fail him; he had been foolish to give them another chance. Disdainful of his hands, he looked out the window. He could still do that, couldn't he? It was raining some now. The landscape started to move, rearing and reeling crazily, as though drunken with the rain. In horror, Didymus damned his eyes. He realized this trouble was probably going to be chronic. He turned his gaze in despair to the trees, to the branches level with his eyes and nearer than the insane ground. Hesitating warily, fearful the gentle boughs under scrutiny would turn into hideous waving tentacles, he looked. With a thrill, he knew he was seeing clearly.

Gauzily rain descended in a fine spray, hanging in fat berries from the wet black branches where leaves had been and buds would be, cold crystal drops. They fell now and then ripely of their own weight, or shaken by the intermittent wind they spilled before their time. Promptly they appeared again, pendulous.

Watching the raindrops prove gravity, he was grateful for nature's, rather than his, return to reason. Still, though he professed faith in his faculties, he would not look away from the trees and down at the ground, nor close his eyes. Gratefully he savored the cosmic truth in the falling drops and the mildly trembling branches. There was order, he thought, which in justice and science ought to include the treacherous landscape. Risking all, he ventured a glance at the ground. All was still there. He smiled. He was going to close his eyes (to make it universal and conclusive), when the door opened again.

Didymus strained to catch the meaning of Titus's movements. Would the clicking sound begin? Titus did go to that corner of the room again. Then it came, louder than before, but only once this time.

Titus came behind his chair, turned it, and wheeled him over to the corner.

On a hook which Titus had screwed into the wall hung a bird cage covered with black cloth.

"What's all this?" Didymus asked.

Titus tapped the covered cage expectantly.

A bird chirped once.

"The bird," Titus explained in excitement, "is inside."

Didymus almost laughed. He sensed in time, however, the necessity of seeming befuddled and severe. Titus expected it.

"I don't believe it," Didymus snapped.

Titus smiled wisely and tapped the cage again.

"There!" he exclaimed when the bird chirped.

Didymus shook his head in mock anger. "You made that beastly noise, Titus, you mountebank!"

Titus, profoundly amused by such skepticism, removed the black cover.

The bird, a canary, flicked its head sidewise in interest, looking them up and down. Then it turned its darting attention to the room. It chirped once in curt acceptance of the new surroundings. Didymus and Titus came under its black dot of an eye once more, this time for closer analysis. The canary chirped twice, perhaps that they were welcome, even pleasing, and stood on one leg to show them what a gay bird it was. It then returned to the business of pecking a piece of apple.

"I see you've given him something to eat," Didymus said, and felt that Titus, though he seemed content to watch the canary, waited for him to say something more. "I am very happy, Titus, to have this canary," he went on. "I suppose he will come in handy now that I must spend my days in this infernal chair."

Titus did not look at him while he said, "He is a good bird, Father. He is one of the Saint's own good birds."

Through the window Didymus watched the days and nights come and go. For the first time, though his life as a friar had been copiously annotated with significant references, he got a good idea of eternity. Monotony, of course, was one word for it, but like all the others, as well as the allegories worked up by imaginative retreat masters, it was empty beside the experience itself, untranslatable. He would doze and wonder if by some quirk he had been cast

out of the world into eternity, but since it was neither
heaven nor exactly purgatory or hell, as he understood
them, he concluded it must be an uncharted isle subscrib-
ing to the mother forms only in the matter of time. And
having thought this, he was faintly annoyed at his ponderous whimsy. Titus, like certain of the hours, came periodically. He would read or simply sit with him in silence.
The canary was there always, but except as it showed signs
of sleepiness at twilight and spirit at dawn, Didymus regarded it as a subtle device, like the days and nights and
bells, to give the lie to the vulgar error that time flies. The
cage was small and the canary would not sing. Time, hanging in the room like a jealous fog, possessed him and
voided everything except it. It seemed impossible each
time Titus came that he should be able to escape the
room.

" 'After him,' " Titus read from Bishop Bale one day,
" 'came Fabius, a Roman born, who (as Eusebius wit-
nesseth) as he was returning home out of the field, and
with his countrymen present to elect a new bishop, there
was a pigeon seen standing on his head and suddenly he
was created pastor of the Church, which he looked not
for.' "

They smiled at having the same thought and both looked
up at the canary. Since Didymus sat by the window most
of the day now, he had asked Titus to put a hook there for
the cage. He had to admit to himself he did this to let
Titus know he appreciated the canary. Also, as a secondary
motive, he reasoned, it enabled the canary to look out the
window. What a little yellow bird could see to interest it in
the frozen scene was a mystery, but that, Didymus sighed,
was a two-edged sword. And he took to watching the canary
more.

So far as he was able to detect the moods of the canary
he participated in them. In the morning the canary, bright
and clownish, flitted back and forth between the two
perches in the cage, hanging from the sides and cocking its
little tufted head at Didymus querulously. During these
acrobatics Didymus would twitch his hands in quick imitation of the canary's stunts. He asked Titus to construct a

tiny swing, such as he had seen, which the canary might learn to use, since it appeared to be an intelligent and daring sort. Titus got the swing, the canary did master it, but there seemed to be nothing Didymus could do with his hands that was like swinging. In fact, after he had been watching awhile, it was as though the canary were fixed to a pendulum, inanimate, a piece of machinery, a yellow blur —ticking, for the swing made a little sound, and Didymus went to sleep, and often when he woke the canary was still going, like a clock. Didymus had no idea how long he slept at these times, maybe a minute, maybe hours. Gradually the canary got bored with the swing and used it less and less. In the same way, Didymus suspected, he himself had wearied of looking out the window. The first meager satisfaction had worn off. The dead trees, the sleeping snow, like the swing for the canary, were sources of diversion which soon grew stale. They were captives, he and the canary, and the only thing they craved was escape. Didymus slowly considered the problem. There was nothing, obviously, for him to do. He could pray, which he did, but he was not sure the only thing wrong with him was the fact he could not walk and that to devote his prayer to that end was justifiable. Inevitably it occurred to him his plight might well be an act of God. Why this punishment, though, he asked himself, and immediately supplied the answer. He had, for one thing, gloried too much in having it in him to turn down Seraphin's request to come to St. Louis. The intention—that was all important, and he, he feared, had done the right thing for the wrong reason. He had noticed something of the faker in himself before. But it was not clear if he had erred. There was a certain consolation, at bottom dismal, in this doubt. It was true there appeared to be a nice justice in being stricken a cripple if he had been wrong in refusing to travel to see Seraphin, if human love was all he was fitted for, if he was incapable of renunciation for the right reason, if the mystic counsels were too strong for him, if he was still too pedestrian after all these years of prayer and contemplation, if . . .

The canary was swinging, the first time in several days. The reality of his position was insupportable. There were two ways of regarding it and he could not make up his mind. Humbly he wished to get well and to be able to walk. But if this was a punishment, was not prayer to lift it declining to see the divine point? He did wish to get well; that would settle it. Otherwise his predicament could only be resolved through means more serious than he dared cope with. It would be like refusing to see Seraphin all over again. By some mistake, he protested, he had at last been placed in a position vital with meaning and precedents inescapably Christian. But was he the man for it? Unsure of himself, he was afraid to go on trial. It would be no minor trial, so construed, but one in which the greatest values were involved—a human soul and the means of its salvation or damnation. Not watered-down suburban precautions and routine pious exercises, but Faith such as saints and martyrs had, and Despair such as only they had been tempted by. No, he was not the man for it. He was unworthy. He simply desired to walk and in a few years to die a normal, uninspired death. He did not wish to see (what was apparent) the greatest significance in his affliction. He preferred to think in terms of physical betterment. He was so sure he was not a saint that he did not consider this easier road beneath him, though attracted by the higher one. That was the rub. Humbly, then, he wanted to be able to walk, but he wondered if there was not presumption in such humility.

Thus he decided to pray for health and count the divine hand not there. Decided. A clean decision—not distinction —no mean feat in the light of all the moral theology he had swallowed. The canary, all its rocking come to naught once more, slept motionless in the swing. Despite the manifest prudence of the course he had settled upon, Didymus dozed off ill at ease in his wheel chair by the window. Distastefully, the last thing he remembered was that "prudence" is a virtue more celebrated in the modern Church.

At his request in the days following a doctor visited him. The Rector came along, too. When Didymus tried to find out the nature of his illness, the doctor looked solemn and pronounced it to be one of those things. Didymus received this with a look of mystification. So the doctor went on to say there was no telling about it. Time alone would tell.

Didymus asked the doctor to recommend some books dealing with cases like his. They might have one of them in the monastery library. Titus could read to him in the meantime. For, though he disliked being troublesome, "one of those things" as a diagnosis meant very little to an unscientific beggar like him. The phrase had a philosophic ring to it, but to his knowledge neither the Early Fathers nor the Scholastics seemed to have dealt with it. The Rector smiled. The doctor, annoyed, replied drily:

"Is that a fact?"

Impatiently Didymus said, "I know how old I am, if that's it."

Nothing was lost of the communion he kept with the canary. He still watched its antics and his fingers in his lap followed them clumsily. He did not forget about himself, that he must pray for health, that it was best that way— "prudence" dictated it—but he did think more of the canary's share of their captivity. A canary in a cage, he reasoned, is like a bud which never blooms.

He asked Titus to get a book on canaries, but nothing came of it and he did not mention it again.

Some days later Titus read:

"'Twenty-ninth pope, Marcellus, a Roman, was pastor of the Church, feeding it with wisdom and doctrine. And (as I may say with the Prophet) a man according to God's heart and full of Christian works. This man admonished Maximianus the Emperor and endeavored to remove him from persecuting the saints——'"

"Stop a moment, Titus," Didymus interrupted.

Steadily, since Titus began to read, the canary had been jumping from the swing to the bottom of the cage and back again. Now it was quietly standing on one foot in the swing. Suddenly it flew at the side of the cage nearest them and hung there, its ugly little claws, like bent wire, hooked to the slender bars. It observed them intently, first Titus and then Didymus, at whom it continued to stare. Didymus's hands were tense in his lap.

"Go ahead, read," Didymus said, relaxing his hands.

"'But the Emperor being more hardened, commanded Marcellus to be beaten with cudgels and to be driven out of the city, wherefore he entered into the house of one Lucina, a widow, and there kept the congregation secretly, which the tyrant hearing, made a stable for cattle of the same house and committed the keeping of it to the bishop Marcellus. After that he governed the Church by writing Epistles, without any other kind of teaching, being condemned to such a vile service. And being thus daily tormented with strife and noisomeness, at length gave up the ghost. Anno 308.'"

"Very good, Titus. I wonder how we missed that one before."

The canary, still hanging on the side of the cage, had not moved, its head turned sidewise, its eye as before fixed on Didymus.

"Would you bring me a glass of water, Titus?"

Titus got up and looked in the cage. The canary hung there, as though waiting, not a feather stirring.

"The bird has water here," Titus said, pointing to the small cup fastened to the cage.

"For me, Titus, the water's for me. Don't you think I know you look after the canary? You don't forget us, though I don't see why you don't."

Titus left the room with a glass.

Didymus's hands were tense again. Eyes on the canary's eye, he got up from his wheel chair, his face strained and white with the impossible effort, and, his fingers somehow managing it, he opened the cage. The canary darted out and circled the room chirping. Before it lit, though it seemed about to make its perch triumphantly the top of the cage, Didymus fell over on his face and lay prone on the floor.

In bed that night, unsuffering and barely alive, he saw at will everything revealed in his past. Events long forgotten happened again before his eyes. Clearly, sensitively, he saw Seraphin and himself, just as they had always been—himself, never quite sure. He heard all that he had ever said, and that anyone had said to him. He had talked too much, too. The past mingled with the present. In the same moment and scene he made his first Communion, was ordained, and confessed his sins for the last time.

The canary perched in the dark atop the cage, head warm under wing, already, it seemed to Didymus, without memory of its captivity, dreaming of a former freedom, an ancestral summer day with flowers and trees. Outside it was snowing.

The Rector, followed by others, came into the room and administered the last sacrament. Didymus heard them all gathered prayerfully around his bed thinking (they thought) secretly: this sacrament often strengthens the dying, tip-of-the-tongue wisdom indigenous to the priesthood, Henry the Eighth had six wives. He saw the same hackneyed smile, designed to cheer, pass bravely among them, and marveled at the crudity of it. They went away then, all except Titus, their individual footsteps sounding (for him) the character of each friar. He might have been Francis himself for what he knew then of the little brothers and the cure of souls. He heard them thinking their expectation to be called from bed before daybreak to return to his room and say the office of the dead over his body, become the body, and whispering hopefully to the contrary. Death was now an unwelcome guest in the cloister.

He wanted nothing in the world for himself at last. This may have been the first time he found his will amenable to the Divine. He had never been less himself and more the saint. Yet now, so close to sublimity, or perhaps only tempted to believe so (the Devil is most wily at the deathbed), he was beset by the grossest distractions. They were to be expected, he knew, as indelible in the order of things: the bingo game going on under the Cross for the seamless garment of the Son of Man: everywhere the sign of the contradiction, and always. When would he cease to be surprised by it? Incidents repeated themselves, twined, parted, faded away, came back clear, and would not be prayed out of mind. He watched himself mounting the pulpit of a metropolitan church, heralded by the pastor as the renowned Franciscan father sent by God in His goodness to preach this novena—like to say a little prayer to test the microphone, Father?—and later reading through the petitions to Our Blessed Mother, cynically tabulating the pleas for a Catholic boy friend, drunkenness banished, the sale of real estate and coming furiously upon one: "that I'm not pregnant." And at the same church on Good Friday carrying the crucifix along the communion rail for the people to kiss, giving them the indulgence, and afterwards in the sacristy wiping the lipstick of the faithful from the image of Christ crucified.

"Take down a book, any book, Titus, and read. Begin anywhere."

Roused by his voice, the canary fluttered, looked sharply about and buried its head once more in the warmth of its wing.

"'By the lions,'" Titus read, "'are understood the acrimonies and impetuosities of the irascible faculty, which faculty is as bold and daring in its acts as are the lions. By the harts and the leaping does is understood the other faculty of the soul, which is the concupiscible—that is—'"

"Skip the exegesis," Didymus broke in weakly. "I can do without that now. Read the verse."

Titus read: "'Birds of swift wing, lions, harts, leaping does, mountains, valleys, banks, waters, breezes, heats and terrors that keep watch by night, by the pleasant lyres and by the siren's song, I conjure you, cease your wrath and touch not the wall . . .'"

"Turn off the light, Titus."

Titus went over to the switch. There was a brief period of darkness during which Didymus's eyes became accustomed to a different shade, a glow rather, which possessed the room slowly. Then he saw the full moon had let down a ladder of light through the window. He could see the snow, strangely blue, falling outside. So sensitive was his mind and eye (because his body, now faint, no longer blurred his vision?) he could count the snowflakes, all of them separately, before they drifted, winding, below the sill.

With the same wonderful clarity, he saw what he had made of his life. He saw himself tied down, caged, stunted in his apostolate, seeking the crumbs, the little pleasure, neglecting the source, always knowing death changes nothing, only immortalizes . . . and still ever lukewarm. In trivial attachments, in love of things, was death, no matter the appearance of life. In the highest attachment only, no matter the appearance of death, was life. He had always known this truth, but now he was feeling it. Unable to move his hand, only his lips, and hardly breathing, was it too late to act?

"Open the window, Titus," he whispered.

And suddenly he could pray. *Hail Mary . . . Holy Mary, Mother of God, pray for us sinners now and at the hour of our death . . .* finally the time to say, *pray for me now—the hour of my death, amen.* Lest he deceive himself at the very end that this was the answer to a lifetime of praying for a happy death, happy because painless, he tried to turn his thoughts from himself, to join them to God, thinking how at last he did—didn't he *now?*—prefer God above all else. But ashamedly not sure he did, perhaps only fearing hell, with an uneasy sense of justice he put himself foremost among the wise in their own generation, the perennials seeking after God when doctor, lawyer, and bank fails. If he wronged himself, he did so out of humility—a holy error. He ended, to make certain he had not fallen under the same old presumption disguised as the face of humility, by flooding his mind with maledictions. He suffered the piercing white voice of the Apocalypse to echo in his soul: *But because thou art lukewarm, and neither cold, nor hot, I will begin to vomit thee out of my mouth.* And St. Bernard, fiery-eyed in a white habit, thundered at him from the twelfth century: "Hell is paved with the bald pates of priests!"

There was a soft flutter, the canary flew to the window sill, paused, and tilted into the snow. Titus stepped too late to the window and stood gazing dumbly after it. He raised a trembling old hand, fingers bent in awe and sorrow, to his forehead, and turned stealthily to Didymus.

Didymus closed his eyes. He let a long moment pass before he opened them. Titus, seeing him awake then, fussed with the window latch and held a hand down to feel the draught, nodding anxiously as though it were the only evil abroad in the world, all the time straining his old eyes for a glimpse of the canary somewhere in the trees.

Didymus said nothing, letting Titus keep his secret. With

his whole will he tried to lose himself in the sight of God, and failed. He was not in the least transported. Even now he could find no divine sign within himself. He knew he still had to look outside, to Titus. God still chose to manifest Himself most in sanctity.

Titus, nervous under his stare, and to account for staying at the window so long, felt for the draught again, frowned, and kept his eye hunting among the trees.

The thought of being the cause of such elaborate dissimulation in so simple a soul made Didymus want to smile —or cry, he did not know which . . . and could do neither. Titus persisted. How long would it be, Didymus wondered faintly, before Titus ungrievingly gave the canary up for lost in the snowy arms of God? The snowflakes whirled at the window, for a moment for all their bright blue beauty as though struck still by lightning, and Didymus closed his eyes, only to find them there also, but darkly falling.

Jamesie

There it was, all about Lefty, in Ding Bell's Dope Box.

"We don't want to add coals to the fire, but it's common knowledge that the Local Pitcher Most Likely To Succeed is fed up with the home town. Well, well, the boy's good, which nobody can deny, and the scouts are on his trail, but it doesn't say a lot for his team spirit, not to mention his civic spirit, this high-hat attitude of his. And that fine record of his—has it been all a case of him and him alone? How about the team? The boys have backed him up, they've given him the runs, and that's what wins ball games. They don't pay off on strike-outs. There's one kind of player every scribe knows—and wishes he didn't—the lad who gets four for four with the willow, and yet, somehow, his team goes down to defeat—but does that worry this gent? Not a bit of it. He's too busy celebrating his own personal success, figuring his batting average, or, if he's a pitcher, his earned run average and strike-outs. The percentage player. We hope we aren't talking about Lefty. If we are, it's too bad, it is, and no matter where he goes from here, especially if it's up to the majors, it won't remain a secret very long, nor will he . . . See you at the game Sunday. Ding Bell."

"Here's a new one, Jamesie," his father said across the porch, holding up the rotogravure section.

With his father on Sunday it could be one of three things —a visit to the office, fixing up his mother's grave in Calvary, or just sitting on the porch with all the Chicago papers, as today.

Jamesie put down the *Courier* and went over to his father without curiosity. It was always Lindy or the *Spirit of St. Louis*, and now without understanding how this could so suddenly be, he was tired of them. His father, who seemed to feel that a growing boy could take an endless interest in these things, appeared to know the truth at last. He gave a page to the floor—that way he knew what he'd read and

how far he had to go—and pulled the newspaper around his
ears again. Before he went to dinner he would put the paper
in order and wish out loud that other people would have
the decency to do the same.

Jamesie, back in his chair, granted himself one more chapter of *Baseball Bill in the World Series*. The chapters were
running out again, as they had so many times before, and
he knew, with the despair of a narcotic, that his need had
no end.

Baseball Bill, at fifty cents a volume and unavailable at
the library, kept him nearly broke, and Francis Murgatroyd,
his best friend . . . too stingy to go halves, confident
he'd get to read them all as Jamesie bought them, and each
time offering to exchange the old Tom Swifts and Don
Sturdys he had got for Christmas—as though that were the
same thing!

Jamesie owned all the Baseball Bills to be had for love
or money in the world, and there was nothing in the back
of this one about new titles being in preparation. Had the
author died, as some of them did, and left his readers in
the lurch? Or had the series been discontinued—for where,
after *Fighting for the Pennant* and *In the World Series*,
could Baseball Bill go? *Baseball Bill, Manager*, perhaps. But
then what?

"A plot to *fix* the World Series! So that was it! Bill began
to see it all. . . . The mysterious call in the night! The
diamond necklace in the dressing room! The scribbled note
under the door! With slow fury Bill realized that the peculiar odor on the note paper was the odor in his room
now! It was the odor of strong drink and cigar smoke! And
it came from his midnight visitor! The same! Did he repre-
sent the powerful gambling syndicate? Was *he* Blackie
Humphrey himself? Bill held his towering rage in check and
smiled at his visitor in his friendly, boyish fashion. His visitor must get no inkling of his true thoughts. Bill must play
the game—play the very fool they took him for! Soon enough
they would discover for themselves, but to their everlasting
sorrow, the courage and daring of Baseball Bill . . ."

Jamesie put the book aside, consulted the batting aver-
ages in the *Courier*, and reread Ding Bell. Then, not wait-

ing for dinner and certain to hear about it at supper, he ate
a peanut butter sandwich with catsup on it, and left by the
back door. He went down the alley calling for Francis Murgatroyd. He got up on the Murgatroyd gate and swung—
the death-defying trapeze act at the circus—until Francis
came down the walk.

"Hello, Blackie Humphrey," Jamesie said tantalizingly.

"Who's Blackie Humphrey?"

"You know who Blackie Humphrey is all right."

"Aw, Jamesie, cut it out."

"And you want me to throw the World Series!"

"Baseball Bill!"

"In the World Series. It came yesterday."

"Can I read it?"

Jamesie spoke in a hushed voice. "So you're Blackie
Humphrey?"

"All right. But I get to read it next."

"So you want me to throw the World Series, Blackie.
Is that it? Say you do."

"Yes, I do."

"Ask me again. Call me Bill."

"Bill, I want you to throw the World Series. Will you,
Bill?"

"I might." But that was just to fool Blackie. Bill tried to
keep his towering rage in check while feigning an interest
in the nefarious plot. "Why do you want me to throw it,
Blackie?"

"I don't know."

"Sure you know. You're a dirty crook and you've got a
lot of dough bet on the other team."

"Uh, huh."

"Go ahead. Tell me that."

While Blackie unfolded the criminal plan Bill smiled at
him in his friendly, boyish fashion.

"And who's behind this, Blackie?"

"I don't know."

"Say it's the powerful gambling syndicate."

"It's them."

"Ah, ha! Knock the ash off your cigar."

"Have I got one?"

"Yes, and you've got strong drink on your breath, too."

"Whew!"

Blackie should have fixed him with his small, piglike eyes.

"Fix me with your small, piglike eyes."

"Wait a minute, Jamesie!"

"Bill. Go ahead. Fix me."

"O.K. But you don't get to be Bill all the time."

"Now blow your foul breath in my face."

"There!"

"Now ask me to have a cigar. Go ahead."

Blackie was offering Bill a cigar, but Bill knew it was to get him to break training and refused it.

"I see through you, Blackie." No, that was wrong. He had to conceal his true thoughts and let Blackie play him for a fool. Soon enough his time would come and . . . "Thanks for the cigar, Blackie," he said. "I thought it was a cheap one. Thanks, I'll smoke it later."

"I paid a quarter for it."

"Hey, that's too much, Francis!"

"Well, if I'm the head of the powerful——"

Mr. Murgatroyd came to the back door and told Francis to get ready.

"I can't go to the game, Jamesie," Francis said. "I have to caddy for him."

Jamesie got a ride with the calliope when it had to stop at the corner for the light. The calliope was not playing now, but yesterday it had roamed the streets, all red and gold and glittering like a hussy among the pious, black Fords parked on the Square, blaring and showing off, with a sign, Jayville vs. Beardstown.

The ball park fence was painted a swampy green except for an occasional new board. Over the single ticket window cut in the fence hung a sign done in the severe black and white railroad manner, "Home of the Jayville Independents," but everybody called them the "Indees."

Jamesie bought a bottle of Green River out of his savings and made the most of it, swallowing it in sips, calling upon his will power under the sun. He returned the bottle and stood for a while by the ticket window making designs in the dust with the corrugated soles of his new tennis shoes. Ding Bell, with a pretty lady on his arm and carrying the black official scorebook, passed inside without paying, and joked about it.

The Beardstown players arrived from sixty miles away with threatening cheers. Their chartered bus stood steaming and dusty from the trip. The players wore gray suits with "Barons" written across their chests and had the names of sponsors on their backs—Palms Café, Rusty's Wrecking, Coca-Cola.

Jamesie recognized some of the Barons but put down a desire to speak to them.

The last man to leave the bus, Jamesie thought, must be Guez, the new pitcher imported from East St. Louis for the game. Ding Bell had it in the Dope Box that "Saliva Joe" was one of the few spitters left in the business, had been up in the Three Eye a few years, was a full-blooded Cuban, and ate a bottle of aspirins a game, just like candy.

The dark pitcher's fame was too much for Jamesie. He walked alongside Guez. He smelled the salt and pepper of the gray uniform, saw the scarred plate on the right toe, saw the tears in the striped stockings—the marks of bravery or moths—heard the distant chomp of tobacco being chewed, felt—almost—the iron drape of the flannel, and was reduced to friendliness with the pitcher, the enemy.

"Are you a real Cuban?"

Guez looked down, rebuking Jamesie with a brief stare, and growled, "Go away."

Jamesie gazed after the pitcher. He told himself that he hated Guez—that's what he did, hated him! But it didn't do much good. He looked around to see if anybody had been watching, but nobody had, and he wanted somebody his size to vanquish—somebody who might think Guez was as good as Lefty. He wanted to bet a million dollars on Lefty against Guez, but there was nobody to take him up on it.

The Indees began to arrive in ones and twos, already in uniform but carrying their spikes in their hands. Jamesie spoke to all of them except J. G. Nickerson, the manager.

J. G. always glared at kids. He thought they were stealing his baseballs and laughing about it behind his back. He was a great one for signaling with a score card from the bench, like Connie Mack, and Ding Bell had ventured to say that managers didn't come any brainier than Jayville's own J. G. Nickerson, even in the big time. But if there should be a foul ball, no matter how tight the game or crucial the situation, J. G. would leap up, straining like a bird dog, and try to place it, waving the bat boy on without taking his eyes off the spot where it disappeared over the fence or in the weeds. That was why they called him the Foul Ball.

The Petersons—the old man at the wheel, a red handkerchief tied tight enough around his neck to keep his head on, and the sons, all players, Big Pete, Little Pete, Middle Pete, and Extra Pete—roared up with their legs hanging out of the doorless Model T and the brass radiator boiling over.

The old man ran the Model T around in circles, damning it for a runaway horse, and finally got it parked by the gate.

"Hold 'er, Knute!" he cackled.

The boys dug him in the ribs, tickling him, and were like puppies that had been born bigger than their father, jollying him through the gate, calling him Barney Oldfield.

Lefty came.

"Hi, Lefty," Jamesie said.

"Hi, kid," Lefty said. He put his arm around Jamesie and took him past the ticket taker.

"It's all right, Mac," he said.

"Today's the day, Lefty," Mac said. "You can do it, Lefty."

Jamesie and Lefty passed behind the grandstand. Jamesie saw Lefty's father, a skinny, brown-faced man in a yellow straw katy.

"There's your dad, Lefty."

Lefty said, "Where?" but looked the wrong way and walked a little faster.

At the end of the grandstand Lefty stopped Jamesie. "My old man is out of town, kid. Got that?"

Jamesie did not see how this could be. He knew Lefty's father. Lefty's father had a brown face and orange gums.

But Lefty ought to know his own father. "I guess it just looked like him, Lefty," Jamesie said.

Lefty took his hand off Jamesie's arm and smiled. "Yeah, that's right, kid. It just looked like him on account of he's out of town—in Peoria."

Jamesie could still feel the pressure of Lefty's fingers on his arm. They came out on the diamond at the Indees bench near first base. The talk quieted down when Lefty appeared. Everybody thought he had a big head, but nobody could say a thing against his pitching record, it was that good. The scout for the New York Yankees had invited him only last Sunday to train with them next spring. The idea haunted the others. J. G. had shut up about the beauties of teamwork.

J. G. was counting the balls when Jamesie went to the suitcase to get one for Lefty. J. G. snapped the lid down.

"It's for Lefty!"

"Huh!"

"He wants it for warm up."

"Did you tell this kid to get you a ball, Left?"

"Should I bring my own?" Lefty said.

J. G. dug into the suitcase for a ball, grunting, "I only asked him." He looked to Jamesie for sympathy. He considered the collection of balls and finally picked out a fairly new one.

"Lefty, he likes 'em brand new," Jamesie said.

"Who's running this club?" J. G. bawled. But he threw the ball back and broke a brand new one out of its box and tissue paper. He ignored Jamesie's ready hand and yelled to Lefty going out to the bull pen, "Coming at you, Left," and threw it wild.

Lefty let the ball bounce through his legs, not trying for it. "Nice throw," he said.

Jamesie retrieved the ball for Lefty. They tossed it back and forth, limbering up, and Jamesie aped Lefty's professional indolence.

When Bugs Bidwell, Lefty's battery mate, appeared with his big mitt, Jamesie stood aside and buttoned his glove back on his belt. Lefty shed his red blanket coat with the leather sleeves and gave it to Jamesie for safekeeping. Jamesie folded it gently over his arm, with the white chenille "J" showing out. He took his stand behind Bugs to get a good look at Lefty's stuff.

Lefty had all his usual stuff—the fast one with the two little hops in it, no bigger than a pea; his slow knuckler that looked like a basketball, all the stitches standing still and staring you in the face; his sinker that started out high like a wild pitch, then dipped a good eight inches and straightened out for a called strike. But something was wrong—Lefty with nothing to say, no jokes, no sudden whoops, was not himself. Only once did he smile at a girl in the bleachers and say she was plenty . . . and sent a fast one smacking into Bug's mitt for what he meant.

That, for a moment, was the Lefty that Jamesie's older cousins knew about. They said a nice kid like Jamesie ought to be kept away from him, even at the ball park. Jamesie was always afraid it would get back to Lefty that the cousins thought he was poor white trash, or that he would know it in some other way, as when the cousins passed him on the street and looked the other way. He was worried, too, about what Lefty might think of his Sunday clothes, the snow-white blouse, the floppy sailor tie, the soft linen pants, the sissy clothes. His tennis shoes—sneakers, he ought to say—were all right, but not the golf stockings that left his knees bare, like a rich kid's. The tough guys, because they were tough or poor—he didn't know which—wore socks, not stockings, and they wore them rolled down slick to their ankles.

Bugs stuck his mitt with the ball in it under his arm and got out his Beechnut. He winked at Jamesie and said, "Chew?"

Jamesie giggled. He liked Bugs. Bugs, on loan from the crack State Hospital team, was all right—nothing crazy about him; he just liked it at the asylum, he said, the big grounds and lots of cool shade, and he was not required to work or take walks like the regular patients. He was the only Indee on speaking terms with Lefty.

Turning to Lefty, Bugs said, "Ever seen this Cuban work?"

"Naw."

"I guess he's got it when he's right."

"That so?" Lefty caught the ball with his bare hand and spun it back to Bugs. "Well, all I can promise you is a no-hit game. It's up to you clowns to get the runs."

"And me hitting a lousy .211."

"All you got to do is hold me. Anyhow what's the Foul Ball want for his five bucks—Mickey Cochrane?"

"Yeah, Left."

"I ought to quit him."

"Ain't you getting your regular fifteen?"

"Yeah, but I ought to quit. The Yankees want me. Is my curve breaking too soon?"

"It's right in there, Left."

It was a pitchers' battle until the seventh inning. Then the Indees pushed a run across.

The Barons got to Lefty for their first hit in the seventh, and when the next man bunted, Lefty tried to field it instead of letting Middle Pete at third have it, which put two on with none out. Little Pete threw the next man out at first, the only play possible, and the runners advanced to second and third. The next hitter hammered a line drive to Big Pete at first, and Big Pete tried to make it two by throwing to second, where the runner was off, but it was too late and the runner on third scored on the play. J. G. from the bench condemned Big Pete for a dumb Swede. The next man popped to short center.

Jamesie ran out with Lefty's jacket. "Don't let your arm get cold, Lefty."

"Some support I got," Lefty said.

"Whyn't you leave me have that bunt, Lefty?" Middle Pete said, and everybody knew he was right.

"Two of them pitches was hit solid," Big Pete said. "Good anywhere."

"Now, boys," J. G. said.

"Aw, dry up," Lefty said, grabbing a blade of grass to chew. "I ought to quit you bums."

Pid Kirby struck out for the Indees, but Little Pete walked, and Middle Pete advanced him to second on a long fly to left. Then Big Pete tripled to the weed patch in center, clear up against the Chevrolet sign, driving in Little

Pete. Guez whiffed Kelly Larkin, retiring the side, and the Indees were leading the Barons 2 to 1.

The first Baron to bat in the eighth had J. G. frantic with fouls. The umpire was down to his last ball and calling for more. With trembling fingers J. G. unwrapped new balls. He had the bat boy and the bat boy's assistant hunting for them behind the grandstand. When one fell among the automobiles parked near first, he started to go and look for himself, but thought of Jamesie and sent him instead. "If anybody tries to hold out on you, come and tell me."

After Jamesie found the ball he crept up behind a familiar blue Hupmobile, dropping to his knees when he was right under Uncle Pat's elbow, and then popping up to scare him.

"Look who's here," his cousin said. It had not been Uncle Pat's elbow at all, but Gabriel's. Uncle Pat, who had never learned to drive, sat on the other side to be two feet closer to the game.

Jamesie stepped up on the running board, and Gabriel offered him some popcorn.

"So you're at the game, Jamesie," Uncle Pat said, grinning as though it were funny. "Gabriel said he thought that was you out there."

"Where'd you get the cap, Jamesie?" Gabriel said.

"Lefty. The whole team got new ones. And if they win today J. G. says they're getting whole new uniforms."

"Not from me," Uncle Pat said, looking out on the field. "Who the thunder's wearing my suit today?"

"Lee Coles, see?" Gabriel said, pointing to the player. Lee's back—Mallon's Grocery—was to them.

Uncle Pat, satisfied, slipped a bottle of near beer up from the floor to his lips and tipped it up straight, which explained to Jamesie the foam on his mustache.

"You went and missed me again this week," Uncle Pat said broodingly. "You know what I'm going to do, Jamesie?"

"What?"

"I'm going to stop taking your old *Liberty* magazine if you don't bring me one first thing tomorrow morning."

"I will." He would have to bring Uncle Pat his own free

copy and erase the crossword puzzle. He never should have
sold out on the street. That was how you lost your regular
customers.

Uncle Pat said, "This makes the second time I started
in to read a serial and had this happen to me."

"Is it all right if the one I bring you tomorrow has got
'Sample Copy' stamped on it?"

"That's all right with me, Jamesie, but I ought to get it
for nothing." Uncle Pat swirled the last inch of beer in the
bottle until it was all suds.

"I like the *Post*," Gabriel said. "Why don't you handle
the *Post*?"

"They don't need anybody now."

"What he ought to handle," Uncle Pat said, "is the
Country Gentleman."

"How's the Rosebud coming, Jamesie?" Gabriel asked.
"But I don't want to buy any."

Uncle Pat and Gabriel laughed at him.

Why was that funny? He'd had to return eighteen boxes
and tell them he guessed he was all through being the local
representative. But why was that so funny?

"Did you sell enough to get the bicycle, Jamesie?"

"No." He had sold all the Rosebud salve he could, but
not nearly enough to get the Ranger bicycle. He had to be
satisfied with the Eveready flashlight.

"Well, I got enough of that Rosebud salve now to grease
the Hup," Gabriel said. "Or to smear all over me the next
time I swim the English Channel—with Gertrude Ederle.
It ought to keep the fishes away."

"It smells nice," Uncle Pat said. "But I got plenty."

Jamesie felt that they were protecting themselves against
him.

"I sent it all back anyway," he said, but that was not
true; there were six boxes at home in his room that he had
to keep in order to get the flashlight. Why was that the
way it always worked out? Same way with the flower seeds.
Why was it that whenever he got a new suit at Meyer Brothers they weren't giving out ball bats or compasses? Why
was it he only won a half pound of bacon at the carnival,
never a Kewpie doll or an electric fan? Why did he always

get tin whistles and crickets in the Crackerjack, never a puzzle, a ring, or a badge? And one time he had got nothing! Why was it that the five-dollar bill he found on South Diamond Street belonged to Mrs. Hutchinson? But he *had* found a quarter in the dust at the circus that nobody claimed.

"Get your aunt Kate to take that cap up in the back," Uncle Pat said, smiling.

Vaguely embarrassed, Jamesie said, "Well, I got to get back."

"If that's Lefty's cap," Gabriel called after him, "you'd better send it to the cleaners."

When he got back to the bench and handed the ball over, J. G. seemed to forget all about the bases being crowded.

"Thank God," he said. "I thought you went home with it."

The Barons were all on Lefty now. Shorty Parker, their manager, coaching at third, chanted, "Take him out . . . Take him out . . . Take him out."

The Barons had started off the ninth with two clean blows. Then Bugs took a foul ball off the chicken wire in front of the grandstand for one out, and Big Pete speared a drive on the rise for another. Two down and runners on first and third. Lefty wound up—bad baseball—and the man on first started for second, the batter stepping into the pitch, not to hit it but to spoil the peg to second. The runner was safe; the man on third, threatening to come home after a false start, slid yelling back into the sack. It was close and J. G. flew off the bench to protest a little.

After getting two strikes on the next batter, Lefty threw four balls, so wide it looked like a deliberate pitchout, and that loaded the bases.

J. G. called time. He went out to the mound to talk it over with Lefty, but Lefty waved him away. So J. G. consulted Bugs behind the plate. Jamesie, lying on the grass a few feet away, could hear them.

"That's the first windup I ever seen a pitcher take with a runner on first."

"It was pretty bad," Bugs said.

"And then walking that last one. He don't look wild to me, neither."

"He ain't wild, J. G.; I'll tell you that."

"I want your honest opinion, Bugs."

"I don't know what to say, J. G."

"Think I better jerk him?"

Bugs was silent, chewing it over.

"Guess I better leave him in, huh?"

"You're the boss, J. G. I don't know nothing for sure."

"I only got Extra Pete to put in. They'd murder him. I guess I got to leave Lefty in and take a chance."

"I guess so."

When J. G. had gone Bugs walked halfway out to the mound and spoke to Lefty. "You all right?"

"I had a little twinge before."

"A little what?"

Lefty touched his left shoulder.

"You mean your arm's gone sore?"

"Naw. I guess it's nothing."

Bugs took his place behind the plate again. He crouched, and Jamesie, from where he was lying, saw two fingers appear below the mitt—the signal. Lefty nodded, wound up, and tried to slip a medium-fast one down the middle. Guez, the batter, poled a long ball into left—foul by a few feet. Bugs shook his head in the mask, took a new ball from the umpire, and slammed it hard at Lefty.

Jamesie saw two fingers below the mitt again. What was Bugs doing? It wasn't smart baseball to give Guez another like the last one!

Guez swung and the ball fell against the left field fence —fair. Lee Coles, the left fielder, was having trouble locating it in the weeds. Kelly Larkin came over from center to help him hunt. When they found the ball, Guez had completed the circuit and the score was 5 to 2 in favor of the Barons.

Big Pete came running over to Lefty from first base, Little Pete from second, Pid Kirby from short, Middle Pete from third. J. G., calling time again, walked out to them.

"C'mere, Bugs," he said.

Bugs came slowly.

"What'd you call for on that last pitch?"

"Curve ball."

"And the one before that?"

"Same."

"And what'd Lefty give you?"

"It wasn't no curve. It wasn't much of anything."

"No," J. G. said. "It sure wasn't no curve ball. It was right in there, not too fast, not too slow, just right—for batting practice."

"It slipped," Lefty said.

"Slipped, huh!" Big Pete said. "How about the other one?"

"They both slipped. Ain't that never happened before?"

"Well, it ain't never going to happen again—not to me, it ain't," J. G. said. "I'm taking you out!"

He shouted to Extra Pete on the bench, "Warm up! You're going in!" He turned to Lefty.

"And I'm firing you. I just found out your old man was making bets under the grandstand—and they wasn't on us! I can put you in jail for this!"

"Try it," Lefty said, starting to walk away.

"If you knew it, J. G.," Big Pete said, "whyn't you let us know?"

"I just now found it out, is why."

"Then I'm going to make up for lost time," Big Pete said, following Lefty, "and punch this guy's nose."

Old man Peterson appeared among them—somebody must have told him what it was all about. "Give it to him, son!" he cackled.

Jamesie missed the fight. He was not tall enough to see over all the heads, and Gabriel, sent by Uncle Pat, was dragging him away from it all.

"I always knew that Lefty was a bad one," Gabriel said on the way home. "I knew it from the time he used to hunch in marbles."

"It reminds me of the Black Sox scandal of 1919," Uncle Pat said. "I wonder if they'll hold the old man, too."

Jamesie, in tears, said, "Lefty hurt his arm and you don't like him just because he don't work, and his father owes

you at the store! Let me out! I'd rather walk by myself
than ride in the Hupmobile—with you!"

He stayed up in his room, feigning a combination stom-
ach-ache and headache, and would not come down for supper. Uncle Pat and Gabriel were down there eating. His
room was over the dining room, and the windows were open
upstairs and down, but he could not quite hear what they
said. Uncle Pat was laughing a lot—that was all for sure—
but then he always did that. Pretty soon he heard no more
from the dining room and he knew they had gone to sit
on the front porch.

Somebody was coming up the stairs. Aunt Kate. He
knew the wavering step at the top of the stairs to be hers,
and the long pause she used to catch her breath—something
wrong with her lungs? Now, as she began to move, he heard
ice tinkling in a glass. Lemonade. She was bringing him
some supper. She knocked. He lay heavier on the bed and
with his head at a painful angle to make her think he was
suffering. She knocked again. If he pinched his forehead it
would look red and feverish. He did. Now.

"Come in," he said weakly.

She came in, gliding across the room in the twilight, tall
and white as a sail in her organdy, serene before her pa-
tient. Not quite opening his eyes, he saw her through the
lashes. She thought he was sick all right, but even if she
didn't, she would never take advantage of him to make a
joke, like Uncle Pat, prescribing, "A good dose of salts!
That's the ticket!" Or Gabriel, who was even meaner, "An
enema!"

He had Aunt Kate fooled completely. He could fool her
every time. On Halloween she was the kind of person who
went to the door every time the bell rang. She was the only
grownup he knew with whom it was not always the teeter-
totter game. She did not raise herself by lowering him. She
did not say back to him the things he said, slightly changed,
accented with a grin, so that they were funny. Uncle Pat
did. Gabriel did. Sometimes, if there was company, his father did.

"Don't you want the shades up, Jamesie?"

She raised the shades, catching the last of that day's sun, bringing the ballplayers on the wall out of the shadows and into action. She put the tray on the table by his bed.

Jamesie sat up and began to eat. Aunt Kate was the best one. Even if she noticed it, she would say nothing about his sudden turn for the better.

She sat across from him in the rocker, the little red one he had been given three years ago, when he was just a kid in the first grade, but she did not look too big for it. She ran her hand over the front of his books, frowning at Baseball Bill, Don Sturdy, Tom Swift, Horatio Alger, Jr., and the *Sporting News*. They had come between him and her.

"Where are the books we used to read, Jamesie?"

"On the bottom shelf."

She bent to see them. There they were, his old friends and hers—hers still. Perseus. Theseus. All those old Greeks. Sir Lancelot. Merlin. Sir Tristram. King Arthur. Oliver Twist. Pinocchio. Gulliver. He wondered how he ever could have liked them, and why Aunt Kate still did. Perhaps he still did, a little. But they turned out wrong, most of them, with all the good guys dying or turning into fairies and the bad guys becoming dwarfs. The books he read now turned out right, if not until the very last page, and the bad guys died or got what was coming to them.

"Were they talking about the game, Aunt Kate?"

"Your uncle was, and Gabriel."

Jamesie waited a moment. "Did they say anything about Lefty?"

"I don't know. Is he the one who lost the game on purpose?"

"That's a lie, Aunt Kate! That's just what Uncle Pat and Gabriel say!"

"Well, I'm sure I don't know——"

"You *are* on their side!"

Aunt Kate reached for his hand, but he drew it back.

"Jamesie, I'm sure I'm not on anyone's side. How can I be? I don't know about baseball—and I don't care about it!"

"Well, I *do*! And I'm not one bit sick—and you thought I was!"

Jamesie rolled out of bed, ran to the door, turned, and said, "Why don't you get out of my room and go and be with them! You're on their side! And Uncle Pat drinks *near beer!*"

He could not be sure, but he thought he had her crying, and if he did it served her right. He went softly down the stairs, past the living room, out the back door, and crept along the house until he reached the front porch. He huddled under the spiraea bushes and listened to them talk. But it was not about the game. It was about President Coolidge. His father was for him. Uncle Pat was against him.

Jamesie crept back along the house until it was safe to stand up and walk. He went down the alley. He called for Francis.

But Francis was not home—still with his father, Mrs. Murgatroyd said.

Jamesie went downtown, taking his own special way, through alleys, across lots, so that he arrived on the Square without using a single street or walking on a single sidewalk. He weighed himself on the scales in front of Kresge's. He weighed eighty-three pounds, and the little card said, "You are the strong, silent type, and silence is golden." He weighed himself in front of Grant's. He weighed eighty-four pounds, and the card said, "Cultivate your good tastes and make the most of your business connections."

He bought a ball of gum from the machine in front of the Owl Drugstore. It looked like it was time for a black one to come out, and black was his favorite flavor, but it was a green one. Anyway he was glad it had not been white.

He coveted the Louisville Sluggers in the window of the D. & M. Hardware. He knew how much they cost. They were autographed by Paul Waner, Ty Cobb, Rogers Hornsby, all the big league stars, and if Lefty ever cracked his, a Paul Waner, he was going to give it to Jamesie, he said.

When Lefty was up with the Yankees—though they had not talked about it yet—he would send for Jamesie. He would make Jamesie the bat boy for the Yankees. He would say to Jake Ruppert, the owner of the Yankees, "Either you hire my friend, Jamesie, as bat boy or I quit." Jake Ruppert would want his own nephew or somebody to have the job, but what could he do? Jamesie would have a uniform like the regular players, and get to travel around the country with them, living in hotels, eating in restaurants, taking taxicabs, and would be known to everybody as Lefty's best friend, and they would both be Babe Ruth's best friends, the three of them going everywhere together. He would get all the Yankees to write their names on an Official American League ball and then send it home to Francis Murgatroyd, who would still be going to school back in Jayville—poor old Francis; and he would write to him on hotel stationery with his own fourteen-dollar fountain pen.

And then he was standing across the street from the jail. He wondered if they had Lefty locked up over there, if Uncle Pat and Gabriel had been right—not about Lefty throwing a game—that was a lie!—but about him being locked up. A policeman came out of the jail. Jamesie waited for him to cross the street. He was Officer Burkey. He was Phil Burkey's father, and Phil had shown Jamesie his father's gun and holster one time when he was sleeping. Around the house Mr. Burkey looked like anybody else, not a policeman.

"Mr. Burkey, is Lefty in there?"

Mr. Burkey, through for the day, did not stop to talk, only saying, "Ah, that he is, boy, and there's where he deserves to be."

Jamesie said "Oh yeah!" to himself and went around to the back side of the jail. It was a brick building, painted gray, and the windows were open, but not so you could see inside, and they had bars over them.

Jamesie decided he could do nothing if Mr. Burkey was off duty. The street lights came on; it was night. He began to wonder, too, if his father would miss him. Aunt Kate would not tell. But he would have to come in the back way and sneak up to his room. If it rained tomorrow he would stay in and make up with Aunt Kate. He hurried home, and did not remember that he had meant to stay out all night, maybe even run away forever.

The next morning Jamesie came to the jail early. Mr. Burkey, on duty, said he might see Lefty for three minutes, but it was a mystery to him why anyone, especially a nice boy like Jamesie, should want to see the bum. "And don't tell your father you were here."

Jamesie found Lefty lying on a narrow iron bed that was all springs and no covers or pillow.

"Lefty," he said, "I came to see you."

Lefty sat up. He blinked at Jamesie and had trouble getting his eyes to see.

Jamesie went closer. Lefty stood up. They faced each other. Jamesie could have put his hand through the bars and touched Lefty.

"Glad to see you, kid."

"Lefty," Jamesie said, "I brought you some reading." He handed Lefty Uncle Pat's copy of *Liberty* magazine.

"Thanks, kid."

He got the box of Rosebud salve out of his pocket for Lefty.

"Well, thanks, kid. But what do I do with it?"

"For your arm, Lefty. It says 'recommended for aches and pains.'"

"I'll try it."

"Do you like oranges, Lefty?"

"I can eat 'em."

He gave Lefty his breakfast orange.

A funny, sweet smell came off Lefty's breath, like perfume, only sour. Burnt matches and cigar butts lay on the cell floor. Did Lefty smoke? Did he? Didn't he realize what it would do to him?

"Lefty, how do you throw your sinker?"

Lefty held the orange and showed Jamesie how he gripped the ball along the seams, how he snapped his wrist before he let it fly.

"But be sure you don't telegraph it, kid. Throw 'em all the same—your fast one, your floater, your curve. Then they don't know where they're at."

Lefty tossed the orange through the bars to Jamesie. "Try it."

Jamesie tried it, but he had it wrong at first, and Lefty

had to reach through the bars and show him again. After that they were silent, and Jamesie thought Lefty did not seem very glad to see him after all, and remembered the last gift.

"And I brought you this, Lefty."

It was *Baseball Bill in the World Series.*

"Yeah?" Lefty said, momentarily angry, as though he thought Jamesie was trying to kid him. He accepted the book reluctantly.

"He's a pitcher, Lefty," Jamesie said. "Like you, only he's a right-hander."

The sour perfume on Lefty's breath came through the bars again, a little stronger on a sigh.

Wasn't that the odor of strong drink and cigar smoke— the odor of Blackie Humphrey? Jamesie talked fast to keep himself from thinking. "This book's all about Baseball Bill and the World Series," he gulped, "and Blackie Humphrey and some dirty crooks that try to get Bill to throw it, but . . ." He gave up; he knew now. And Lefty had turned his back.

After a moment, during which nothing happened inside him to explain what he knew now, Jamesie got his legs to take him away, out of the jail, around the corner, down the street—away. He did not go through alleys, across lots, between buildings, over fences. No. He used the streets and sidewalks, like anyone else, to get where he was going— away—and was not quite himself.

He Don't Plant Cotton

Spring entered the black belt in ashes, dust, and drabness, without benefit of the saving green. The seasons were known only by the thermometer and the clothing of the people. There were only a few nights in the whole year when the air itself told you. Perhaps a night in April or May might escape the plague of smells, achieve a little of the enchantment, be the diminished echo of spring happening ardently in the suburbs, but it was all over in a night and the streets were filled with summer, as a hollow mouth with bad breath, and even the rain could not wash it away. And winter . . .

The beginning snow swirled in from the lake, dusting the streets with white. Baby squinted down the lonesome tracks. The wind twisted snow into his eyes, the flakes as sharp as sand, grinding, and his eyeballs were coated with cold tears. Baby worked his hands in his overcoat pockets to make heat. He saw a woman cross the street to catch the Big Red, which was coming now, but the woman refused stiffly to run for it. The wind went off hooting down the tracks ahead. Baby got on. The conductor held out one hand for the fare and yanked a cord twice with the other, prodding the red monster into motion.

Baby sat down inside. A cold breeze swept the floor, rattling old transfers and gum wrappers. Baby placed his feet uneasily on the heater to make the meager warmth funnel up his pants' legs. The dark flesh beneath the tuxedo was chilled to chalky gray at the joints. He listened to the wheels bump over the breaks in the track, and the warmth from the heater rose higher on his legs. He became warm and forgetful of the weather, except as scenery. The streets were paved evenly with snow twinkling soft and clean and white under the lights, and velvet red and green from the neon signs.

New York may be all right, he hummed to himself, but Beale Street's paved with gold. That's a lie, he thought; I been down on Beale. And Chicago, same way. All my life playing jobs in Chicago, and I still got to ride the Big Red. And that's no lie. Jobs were getting harder and harder to find. What they wanted was Mickey Mouse sound effects, singing strings, electric guitars, neon violins, even organs and accordions and harmonica teams. Hard to find a spot to play in, and when you did it was always a white place with drunken advertising men wanting to hear "a old song"—"My Wild Irish Rose" or "I Love You Truly." So you played it, of course, and plenty of schmaltz. And the college kids who wanted swing—any slick popular song. So you played that, too. And always you wanted to play the music you were born to, blue or fast, music that had no name. You managed somehow to play that, too, when there was a lull or the place was empty and you had to stay until 4 A.M. anyway.

Baby got off the streetcar and walked the same two blocks he saw every night except Tuesday. The wind had died down almost entirely and the snow whirled in big flakes end over end. Padding along, Baby told himself he liked winter better than summer. Then he came to the place, said, "How's it, Chief?" to the doorman, an Indian passing for Negro, went down three steps, and forgot all about winter and summer. It was always the same here. It was not so much a place of temperatures as a place of lights and shades and chromium, pastel mirrors, the smell of beer, rum, whisky, smoke—a stale blend of odors and shadows, darkness and music. It was a place of only one climate and that was it.

Baby's overcoat, hat, and scarf went into a closet and settled familiarly on hooks. His old tuxedo walked over to the traps. Its black hands rubbed together briskly, driving out the chill. One hand fumbled in the dark at the base of the big drum, and a second later a watery blue light winked on dully and flooded the drumhead, staring like a blind blue eye. Immediately the tuxedo sat down and worked its feet with a slight rasping noise into the floor. The fingers thumped testingly on the hide, tightened the snare. They knew, like the ears, when it was right. Gingerly, as always, the right foot sought the big drum's pedal. The tuxedo was not ready yet. It had to fidget and massage its seat around on the chair, stretch out its arms, and hug the whole outfit a fraction of an inch this way and that. Then the eyes glanced at the piano player, signaling ready. The drumsticks paused a moment tensely, slid into the beat, barely heard, accenting perfectly the shower of piano notes. Everything worked together for two choruses. Then the piano player tapered his solo gently, so that at a certain point Baby knew it was his. He brought the number to a lifeless close, run down. Too early in the evening.

"Dodo," Baby said to the piano player, "Libby come in yet?"

Dodo sent a black hand up, slow as smoke, toward the ceiling. "Upstairs," he said, letting the hand fall to the keyboard with a faint, far-off chord. It stirred there, gently worming music from the battered upright. Notes drew nearer, riding on ships and camels through a world of sand and water, till they came forthright from the piano, taking on patterns, as the other black hand came to life on the bass keys, dear to Dodo. Baby picked up his sticks, recognizing the number. He called it "Dodo's Blues," though he knew Dodo called it nothing. Every night about this time, when there was no crowd and Dodo hadn't yet put on the white coat he wore servicing the bar, they would play it. Baby half closed his eyes. With pleasure he watched Dodo through the clouds of rhythm he felt shimmering up like heat from his drums. Baby's eyes were open only enough to frame Dodo like a picture; everything else was out. It was a picture of many dimensions; music was only one of them.

Here was a man, midgety, hunchbacked, black, and proud—mostly all back and music. A little man who, when he was fixing to play, had to look around for a couple of three-inch telephone directories. Piling them on top of the piano bench, he sat down, with all their names and streets and numbers and exchanges under him. He had very little of thighs and stomach—mostly just back, which threw a round shadow on the wall. When he leaned farther away from the piano, so the light slanted through his hands, his shadow revealed him walking on his hands down the keyboard, dancing on the tips of fingery toes. Sometimes it seemed to Baby through half-closed eyes, when Dodo's body was bobbing on the wall and his hands were feet dancing on the keyboard, as though the dim light shaped him into a gigantic, happy spider. When he became a spider you could forget he was a man, hunchbacked, runt-ish, black; and he, too, could forget perhaps that he had to be careful and proud. Perhaps he could be happy always if his back and size and color and pride were not always standing in the way. The piano made him whole. The piano taught him to find himself and jump clean over the moon. When he played, his feet never touched the pedals.

People were beginning to fill the place. They finished off the number, Baby smiling his admiration, Dodo scrupulously expressionless.

"For a young man . . ." Baby said.

Dodo got down off the telephone directories and threw them under the piano at the bass end, beyond the blue glow of the big drum. He had seen Libby come down the steps from the dressing room—a red dress, a gardenia. Dodo went behind the bar and put on his white service coat. Libby sat down at the piano.

Helplessly attracted, several men came over from the bar and leaned on the piano. They stared, burdening Libby's body with calculations. Singly at first and then, gathering unity, together. Libby sang a popular song. The men went back to the bar to get their drinks, which they brought over and set on top of the upright. Libby sang the words about lost love, and the men licked their lips vacantly. At the end of the song they clapped fiercely. Libby ignored them with a smile.

"Say, that was just fine," one man said. "Where you from anyhow?"

With a little grin Libby acknowledged Baby. Baby, beaming his veteran admiration of a fine young woman, nodded.

"Where you from? Huh?"

"New Orleans."

"Well, you don't say!" the man blurted out joyfully. "We're from down South, too . . . Mississippi, matter of fact!"

Icily, Libby smiled her appreciation of this coincidence. She looked at Baby, who was also registering appropriately. Just think of that! Small world! And welcome to our city!

"Well, what do you know!" crowed the gentleman from Mississippi. "So you're from down South!" He was greatly pleased and already very drunk. He eyed his friends, four or five of them, distributing his discovery equally among them.

"You never know," he explained. Then he appeared to suffer a pang of doubt. He turned quickly to Libby again, as though to make sure she was still there. His eyes jellied blearily and in them an idea was born.

"I know," he said. "Sing . . . sing—sing 'Ol' Man River' for the boys. They all'd sure like that."

Without responding, Libby looked down at her hands, smiling. She measured chords between her thumbs and little fingers, working her amusement into the keys. Baby stared at the mottled hide of his snare drum, at the big one's rim worn down from playing "Dixieland." The gentleman from Mississippi got worried.

"Aw, sing it," he pleaded. So Libby sang a chorus. The gentlemen from Mississippi were overwhelmed. They loved the song, they loved the South, the dear old Southland. Land of cotton, cinnamon seed, and sandy bottom. Look away! Look away! They loved themselves. Look away! Look away! There was the tiniest touch of satire in Libby's voice, a slightly overripe fervor. Baby caught it and behind the bar Dodo caught it, but the gentlemen did not. Dodo had put down the martini glass he was polishing and look away! look away!—good.

At the bridge of the second chorus, Libby nodded "Take it!" to Baby. He stood up, staggering from the heat of the fields, clenching his black, toilworn fists. In profound anguish, he hollered, giving the white folks his all, really knocking himself out.

> *"Tote dat barge*
> *Lift dat bale*
> *Git a little drunk—"*

Baby grimaced in torment and did his best to look like ol' Uncle Tom out snatchin' cotton.

Behind the bar, unnoticed, Dodo's sad black face had turned beatific. "—And you land in jail!" Dodo could not see the other faces, the big white ones, but he could imagine them, the heads fixed and tilted. It was too dark in the place, and he could make out only blurrily the outlines of the necks. Ordinarily he was capable only of hating them. Now he had risen to great unfamiliar heights and was actually enjoying them. Surprised at this capacity in himself, yet proud he could feel this way, he was confused. He went further and started to pity them. But his memory stood up outraged at his forgetfulness and said, Kill that pity dead. Then he remembered he was really alone in the place. It was different with Libby and Baby, though they were black, too. He did not understand why. Say their skin was thicker—only that was not why. Probably this was not the first time they had jived white folks to death and them none the wiser. Dodo was not like that; he had to wait a long time for his kicks. From his heart no pity went out for the white men. He kept it all to himself, where it was needed. But he had to smile inside of him with Libby and Baby. Only more. Look at that fool Baby! Jam up!

> *"Bend yo' knees*
> *An' bow yo' head*
> *An' pull dat rope*
> *Until yo're dead."*

Baby sat down with a thud, exhausted. The gentlemen from Mississippi brayed their pleasure. My, it was good to see that black boy all sweatin' and perspirin' that way. They clapped furiously, called for drinks, gobbled . . .

"And bring some for the darkies!"

Baby swallowed some of his drink. He looked at the

beaten rim of the big drum, then at the sticks. He took out his pocketknife and scraped the rough, splintery places smooth. He glanced at Libby and ventured the kind of smile he felt and knew she did. He finished his drink. The gentlemen from Mississippi hung around the piano, getting drunker, shouting in one another's faces. Nervously Libby lighted a cigarette. A college boy tried to make conversation with her while his honey-haired girl assumed an attitude of genuine concern.

"Can you play 'Hot Lips'?" He was the real American Boy.

"Don't know it," Libby lied. She wished she didn't.

"Can you play 'Sugar Blues'?" Right back.

"Don't know it."

One of the Mississippi gentlemen, who had been hanging back, crowded up to the piano, making his move. He drained his drink and pushed closer to the piano so as to brush Libby's left hand with the front of his trousers. Libby moved her hand, sounding a chord that Baby caught. The gentleman, grinning lewdly, tried to follow her hand up the keyboard.

"That's all right," he snickered. "Play lots of bass, honey."

The first gentleman from Mississippi, drink in hand, stumbled over from the bar. He told Libby to play that "Ol' Man River" song some more. Libby hesitated. Then she lit into it, improvising all around it, and it was a pleasure for Baby, but the first gentleman from Mississippi was not happy. He said if that was the best she could do she had better try singing. Libby sang only one chorus. The gentlemen from Mississippi, though they applauded, were not gratified. There was an air of petulance among them. They remembered another time they heard the song, but it was not clear now what had made it different and better. They saw Baby all right, but they did not remember that he was the one who had sung before, the good one that toted their bars, lifted their bales, and landed drunk in their jails. Something was wrong, but they saw no remedy. Each gentleman suspected the fault was personal, what with him drinking so heavy and all.

Dodo, behind the bar, had not enjoyed the song the last time, hating the coercion the white men worked on Libby and Baby, and feared his advantage was slipping away. In a minute he would be hating them to pieces again.

"Can you play 'Tiger Rag'?" The American Boy was back.

"No." Libby made a face and then managed to turn it into a smile for him. He held his drink up for the world to see on the night before the big game.

The honey-haired girl wrenched her face into a winning smile and hit the jack pot. "Can you play 'St. Louis Blues'?"

"How you want it?" Libby said. She put out her cigarette. "Blues, rhumba . . . what kind a way?"

"Oh, play it low down. The way *you people* play it." So Libby would understand, she executed a ponderous wink, narrowed her eyes, and made them glitter wantonly behind the lashes. "*You* know," she said.

Libby knew. She played "St. Louis," losing herself in it with Baby. She left the college boy and the honey-haired girl behind. She forgot she knew. She gazed at Baby with her eyes dreamy, unseeing, blind with the blue drum, her head nodding in that wonderful, graceful way. Baby saw his old tuxedo in the mirror, its body shimmying on the chair, and he was pleased. The drums, beating figures, rocked with a steady roll. They were playing "Little Rock Getaway" now, the fine, young-woman music.

And Libby was pleased, watching Baby. And then, somehow, he vanished for her into the blue drum. The sticks still danced at an oblique angle on the snare, but there were no hands to them and Libby could not see Baby on the chair. She could only feel him somewhere in the blue glow. Abandoning herself, she lost herself in the piano. Now, still without seeing him, she could feel him with a clarity and warmth beyond vision. Miniature bell notes, mostly blue, blossomed ecstatically, perished *affettuoso*, weaving themselves down into the dark beauty of the lower keys, because it was closer to the drum, and multiplied. They came back to "St. Louis" again.

"Stop." The first gentleman from Mississippi touched

Libby on the arm. "When I do that to you, that means 'Stop,'" he said. Libby chorded easily. "Some of the boys like to hear that 'Ol' Man River' some more." He straightened up, turning to the other gentlemen, his smile assuring them it would not be long now.

"Kick off," Baby sighed.

But Libby broke into "St. Louis" again. Baby, with a little whoop, came clambering after, his sticks slicing into the drum rim, a staccato "Dixieland."

The first gentleman frowned, touching Libby's arm, "Remember what that means? Means 'Ol' Man River,'" he said calmly, as though correcting a slight error. "Toot sweet. Know what that means? That's French. Means right now." No harm done, however. Just that his friends here, a bunch of boys from down South, were dying to hear that song again—up to him to see that they got satisfaction—knew there would be no trouble about it.

"We'll play it for you later on," Libby said quickly. "We got some other requests besides yours. How many you got now, Baby?"

Baby held up eight fingers, very prompt.

"Coming up," he said.

The first gentleman was undecided. "Well . . ." he drawled. Libby began a popular song. The first gentleman faced his friends. His eyes more or less met theirs and found no agreement. The boys looked kind of impatient, like a bunch of boys out for a little fun and not doing so well. He turned to Libby again.

"We just gotta have that 'Ol' Man River' some more. Boys all got their hearts set on it," he said. "Right away! Toot sweet! Toot—away!" There he'd gone and made a joke, and the boys all laughed and repeated it to each other. Libby played on, as though she had not heard. The first gentleman took hold of her arm. She gazed steadily up into his bleary eyes.

"Not now. Later."

"No, you don't. You gotta play it right now. For a bunch of boys from down South. They all got a hankerin' to hear that 'Ol' Man River' some more."

"So you best play it," another gentleman said, leaning

down hard on the old upright piano. "On account of I'm gonna take and give ear. We kinda like how that old song sounds up North. Whatcha all need. The drummer will sing," he said, and looked at Baby. Baby looked back, unsmiling.

Libby chorded lightly, waiting for the gentlemen from Mississippi to get tired. They could not see how it was with her and Baby—never.

"You ain't gonna play?"

Baby's eyes strained hard in their sockets.

"We ain't comin'," Libby said.

Baby's eyes relaxed and he knew the worst part was over. They felt the same way about it. They had made up their minds. The rest was easy. Baby was even a little glad it had happened. A feeling was growing within him that he had wanted to do this for a long time—for years and years, in a hundred different places he had played.

Secretly majestic, Baby sat at his drums, the goal of countless uplifted eyes—beseeching him. For it seemed that hordes of white people were far below him, making their little commotions and noises, asking favors of him, like Lord, please bring the rain, or Lord, please take it away. Lord Baby. Waves of warm exhilaration washed into him, endearing him to himself. No, he smiled, I am sorry, no favors today. Yes, Lord, they all said, if that's the way it is, so be it.

But somebody objected. The manager's voice barked, far below, scarcely audible to Baby in his new eminence. ". . . honoring requests," he heard, and ". . . trouble with the local," and ". . . wanting to get a sweet-swing trio in this place a long time now." And the manager, strangely small, an excited, pale pygmy, explaining to the gentlemen from Mississippi, also small, how it was, "That's all I can do in the circumstances," and them saying, "Well, I guess so; well, I guess so all right; don't pay to pamper 'em, to give 'em an inch."

Baby noticed Libby had got up from the piano and put on her coat, the long dress hanging out at the bottom, red.

"I won't change," she said, and handed Baby the canvas cover for the snare drum.

"Huh?" Baby said foggily. He set about taking his traps apart. Dodo, not wearing his white service coat, came over to help.

"You don't have to," Baby said.

Chief, freezing outside in his long, fancy maroon coat, opened the door for them. "You all through, Baby?"

"Yeah, Chief. You told that right."

They walked down the street toward the car line. Baby, going first, plowed a path for Libby and Dodo in the snow. Window sills, parked cars, and trees were padded with it. The wind was dead and buried. Baby bore the big drum on his shoulder and felt the sticks pressing tight and upright in his vest pockets, two on each side. Libby had her purse and street clothes rolled up under her arm. Dodo carried the snare drum.

Softly as snow, Libby laughed, "That's all I can do in the circumstances," she said.

"I got your old circumstances," Baby said.

Then they were silent, tramping in the snow.

At the corner they waited in a store entrance for a south-bound streetcar. Libby raised a foot now and then, shuddering with cold. Dead still, Dodo breathed down inside the collar of his overcoat, retarding his breath, frowning at the little smoke trickling out, as though it were the only thing left in the world to remind him he was alive. Baby talked of taking a cab and finally did go out into the street to hail one approaching. It slowed up, pulled over to the curb, hesitated . . . and lurched away, with Baby's hand reaching for the door. Baby watched the cab speed down the snowy street, following it for a few steps, speechless. There was nothing to do. Without looking, he saw Libby and Dodo shivering in the store entrance. They had seen the cab come and go. They had not moved an inch. They waited unfooled, as before, for the Big Red.

"What's wrong with you, Baby?" Libby called out. A tiny moment of silence, and she was laughing, gradually louder, mellow octaves of it, mounting, pluming . . .

Like her piano, it seemed to Baby—that fine, young-woman laughter.

"Why you laugh so much, woman?" he inquired plain-

tively from the street. Then he moved to join them, a few
steps only, dallying at the curb to temper the abruptness
of his retreat. Like her piano on "Little Rock"—that fine,
young-woman laughter.

The Forks

That summer when Father Eudex got back from saying
Mass at the orphanage in the morning, he would park Monsignor's car, which was long and black and new like a poli-
tician's, and sit down in the cool of the porch to read his
office. If Monsignor was not already standing in the door,
he would immediately appear there, seeing that his car had
safely returned, and inquire:

"Did you have any trouble with her?"

Father Eudex knew too well the question meant, Did
you mistreat my car?

"No trouble, Monsignor."

"Good," Monsignor said, with imperfect faith in his curate, who was not a car owner. For a moment Monsignor
stood framed in the screen door, fumbling his watch fob
as for a full-length portrait, and then he was suddenly not
there.

"Monsignor," Father Eudex said, rising nervously, "I've
got a chance to pick up a car."

At the door Monsignor slid into his frame again. His
face expressed what was for him intense interest.

"Yes? Go on."

"I don't want to have to use yours every morning."

"It's all right."

"And there are other times." Father Eudex decided not
to be maudlin and mention sick calls, nor be entirely honest
and admit he was tired of busses and bumming rides from
parishioners. "And now I've got a chance to get one—
cheap."

Monsignor, smiling, came alert at *cheap*.

"New?"

"No, I wouldn't say it's new."

Monsignor was openly suspicious now. "What kind?"

"It's a Ford."

"And not new?"

"Not new, Monsignor—but in good condition. It was owned by a retired farmer and had good care."

Monsignor sniffed. He *knew* cars. "V-Eight, Father?"

"No," Father Eudex confessed. "It's a Model A."

Monsignor chuckled as though this were indeed the damnedest thing he had ever heard.

"But in very good condition, Monsignor."

"You said that."

"Yes. And I could take it apart if anything went wrong. My uncle had one."

"No doubt." Monsignor uttered a laugh at Father Eudex's rural origins. Then he delivered the final word, long delayed out of amusement. "It wouldn't be prudent, Father. After all, this isn't a country parish. You know the class of people we get here."

Monsignor put on his Panama hat. Then, apparently mistaking the obstinacy in his curate's face for plain ignorance, he shed a little more light. "People watch a priest, Father. *Damnant quod non intelligunt.* It would never do. You'll have to watch your tendencies."

Monsignor's eyes tripped and fell hard on the morning paper lying on the swing where he had finished it.

"Another flattering piece about that crazy fellow. . . . There's a man who might have gone places if it weren't for his mouth! A bishop doesn't have to get mixed up in all that stuff!"

Monsignor, as Father Eudex knew, meant unions, strikes, race riots—all that stuff.

"A parishioner was saying to me only yesterday it's getting so you can't tell the Catholics from the Communists, with the priests as bad as any. Yes, and this fellow is the worst. He reminds me of that bishop a few years back—at least he called himself a bishop, a Protestant—that was advocating companionate marriages. It's not that bad, maybe, but if you listened to some of them you'd think that Catholicity and capitalism were incompatible!"

"The Holy Father——"

"The Holy Father's in Europe, Father. Mr. Memmers lives in this parish. I'm his priest. What can I tell him?"

"Is it Mr. Memmers of the First National, Monsignor?"

"It is, Father. And there's damned little cheer I can give a man like Memmers. Catholics, priests, and laity alike —yes, and princes of the Church, all talking atheistic communism!"

This was the substance of their conversation, always, the deadly routine in which Father Eudex played straight man. Each time it happened he seemed to participate, and though he should have known better he justified his participation by hoping that it would not happen again, or in quite the same way. But it did, it always did, the same way, and Monsignor, for all his alarms, had nothing to say really and meant one thing only, the thing he never said—that he dearly wanted to be, and was not, a bishop.

Father Eudex could imagine just what kind of bishop Monsignor would be. His reign would be a wise one, excessively so. His mind was made up on everything, excessively so. He would know how to avoid the snares set in the path of the just man, avoid them, too, in good taste and good conscience. He would not be trapped as so many good shepherds before him had been trapped, poor souls —caught in fair-seeming dilemmas of justice that were best left alone, like the first apple. It grieved him, he said, to think of those great hearts broken in silence and solitude. It was the worst kind of exile, alas! But just give him the chance and he would know what to do, what to say, and, more important, what not to do, not to say—neither yea nor nay for him. He had not gone to Rome for nothing. For him the dark forest of decisions would not exist; for him, thanks to hours spent in prayer and meditation, the forest would vanish as dry grass before fire, his fire. He knew the mask of evil already—birth control, indecent movies, salacious books—and would call these things by their right names and dare to deal with them for what they were, these new occasions for the old sins of the cities of the plains.

But in the meantime—oh, to have a particle of the faith that God had in humanity! Dear, trusting God forever trying them beyond their feeble powers, ordering terrible tests, fatal trials by nonsense (the crazy bishop). And keeping Monsignor steadily warming up on the side lines, ready to rush in, primed for the day that would perhaps never dawn.

At one time, so the talk went, there had been reason to think that Monsignor was headed for a bishopric. Now it was too late; Monsignor's intercessors were all dead; the cupboard was bare; he knew it at heart, and it galled him to see another man, this *crazy* man, given the opportunity, and making such a mess of it.

Father Eudex searched for and found a little salt for Monsignor's wound. "The word's going around he'll be the next archbishop," he said.

"I won't believe it," Monsignor countered hoarsely. He glanced at the newspaper on the swing and renewed his horror. "If that fellow's right, Father, I'm"—his voice cracked at the idea—"*wrong!*"

Father Eudex waited until Monsignor had started down the steps to the car before he said, "It could be."

"I'll be back for lunch, Father. I'm taking her for a little spin."

Monsignor stopped in admiration a few feet from the car—her. He was as helpless before her beauty as a boy with a birthday bicycle. He could not leave her alone. He had her out every morning and afternoon and evening. He was indiscriminate about picking people up for a ride in her. He kept her on a special diet—only the best of gas and oil and grease, with daily rubdowns. He would run her only on the smoothest roads and at so many miles an hour. That was to have stopped at the first five hundred, but only now, nearing the thousand mark, was he able to bring himself to increase her speed, and it seemed to hurt him more than it did her.

Now he was walking around behind her to inspect the tires. Apparently O.K. He gave the left rear fender an amorous chuck and eased into the front seat. Then they drove off, the car and he, to see the world, to explore each other further on the honeymoon.

Father Eudex watched the car slide into the traffic, and waited, on edge. The corner cop, fulfilling Father Eudex's fears, blew his whistle and waved his arms up in all four directions, bringing traffic to a standstill. Monsignor pulled expertly out of line and drove down Clover Boulevard in a one-car parade; all others stalled respectfully. The cop, as Monsignor passed, tipped his cap, showing a bald head. Monsignor, in the circumstances, could not acknowledge him, though he knew the man well—a parishioner. He was occupied with keeping his countenance kindly, grim, and exalted, that the cop's faith remain whole, for it was evidently inconceivable to him that Monsignor should ever venture abroad unless to bear the Holy Viaticum, always racing with death.

Father Eudex, eyes baleful but following the progress of the big black car, saw a hand dart out of the driver's window in a wave. Monsignor would combine a lot of business with pleasure that morning, creating what he called "good will for the Church"—all morning in the driver's seat toasting passers-by with a wave that was better than a blessing. How he loved waving to people!

Father Eudex overcame his inclination to sit and stew about things by going down the steps to meet the mailman. He got the usual handful for the Monsignor—advertisements and amazing offers, the unfailing crop of chaff from dealers in church goods, organs, collection schemes, insurance, and sacramental wines. There were two envelopes addressed to Father Eudex, one a mimeographed plea from a missionary society which he might or might not acknowledge with a contribution, depending upon what he thought of the cause—if it was really lost enough to justify a levy on his poverty—and the other a check for a hundred dollars.

The check came in an eggshell envelope with no explanation except a tiny card, "Compliments of the Rival Tractor Company," but even that was needless. All over town clergymen had known for days that the checks were on the way again. Some, rejoicing, could hardly wait. Father Eudex, however, was one of those who could.

With the passing of hard times and the coming of the fruitful war years, the Rival Company, which was a great one for public relations, had found the best solution to the excess-profits problem to be giving. Ministers and even rabbis shared in the annual jack pot, but Rival employees were largely Catholic and it was the checks to the priests that paid off. Again, some thought it was a wonderful idea, and others thought that Rival, plagued by strikes and justly so, had put their alms to work.

There was another eggshell envelope, Father Eudex saw, among the letters for Monsignor, and knew his check would be for two hundred, the premium for pastors.

Father Eudex left Monsignor's mail on the porch table by his cigars. His own he stuck in his back pocket, wanting to forget it, and went down the steps into the yard. Walking back and forth on the shady side of the rectory where the lilies of the valley grew and reading his office, he gradually drifted into the back yard, lured by a noise. He came upon Whalen, the janitor, pounding pegs into the ground.

Father Eudex closed the breviary on a finger. "What's it all about, Joe?"

Joe Whalen snatched a piece of paper from his shirt and handed it to Father Eudex. "He gave it to me this morning."

He—it was the word for Monsignor among them. A docile pronoun only, and yet when it meant the Monsignor it said, and concealed, nameless things.

The paper was a plan for a garden drawn up by the Monsignor in his fine hand. It called for a huge fleur-de-lis bounded by smaller crosses—and these Maltese—a fountain, a sundial, and a cloister walk running from the rectory to the garage. Later there would be birdhouses and a ten-foot wall of thick gray stones, acting as a moat against the eyes of the world. The whole scheme struck Father Eudex as expensive and, in this country, Presbyterian.

When Monsignor drew the plan, however, he must have been in his medieval mood. A spouting whale jostled with Neptune in the choppy waters of the fountain. North was indicated in the legend by a winged cherub huffing and puffing.

Father Eudex held the plan up against the sun to see the watermark. The stationery was new to him, heavy, simulated parchment, with the Church of the Holy Redeemer and Monsignor's name embossed, three initials,

W. F. X., William Francis Xavier. With all those initials
the man could pass for a radio station, a chancery wit had
observed, or if his last name had not been Sweeney, Father Eudex added now, for high Anglican.

Father Eudex returned the plan to Whalen, feeling sorry
for him and to an extent guilty before him—if only because he was a priest like Monsignor (now turned archi-
tect) whose dream of a monastery garden included the
overworked janitor under the head of "labor."

Father Eudex asked Whalen to bring another shovel. Together, almost without words, they worked all morning
spading up crosses, leaving the big fleur-de-lis to the last.
Father Eudex removed his coat first, then his collar, and
finally was down to his undershirt.

Toward noon Monsignor rolled into the driveway.

He stayed in the car, getting red in the face, recovering
from the pleasure of seeing so much accomplished as he
slowly recognized his curate in Whalen's helper. In a still,
appalled voice he called across the lawn, "Father," and
waited as for a beast that might or might' not have
sense enough to come.

Father Eudex dropped his shovel and went over to the
car, shirtless.

Monsignor waited a moment before he spoke, as though
annoyed by the everlasting necessity, where this person was
concerned, to explain. "Father," he said quietly at last, "I
wouldn't do any more of that—if I were you. Rather, in
any event, I wouldn't."

"All right, Monsignor."

"To say the least, it's not prudent. If necessary"—he
paused as Whalen came over to dig a cross within earshot
—"I'll explain later. It's time for lunch now."   ·

The car, black, beautiful, fierce with chromium, was
quiet as Monsignor dismounted, knowing her master. Monsignor went around to the rear, felt a tire, and probed a
nasty cinder in the tread.

"Look at that," he said, removing the cinder.

Father Eudex thought he saw the car lift a hoof, gaze
around, and thank Monsignor with her headlights.

Monsignor proceeded at a precise pace to the back door

of the rectory. There he held the screen open momentarily, as if remembering something or reluctant to enter before himself—such was his humility—but then called to Whalen with an intimacy that could never exist between them.

"Better knock off now, Joe."

Whalen turned in on himself. "*Joe*—is it!"

Father Eudex removed his clothes from the grass. His hands were all blisters, but in them he found a little absolution. He apologized to Joe for having to take the afternoon off. "I can't make it, Joe. Something turned up."

"Sure, Father."

Father Eudex could hear Joe telling his wife about it that night—yeah, the young one got in wrong with the old one again. Yeah, the old one, he don't believe in it, work, for them.

Father Eudex paused in the kitchen to remember he knew not what. It was in his head, asking to be let in, but he did not place it until he heard Monsignor in the next room complaining about the salad to the housekeeper. It was the voice of dear, dead Aunt Hazel, coming from the summer he was ten. He translated the past into the present: I can't come out and play this afternoon, Joe, on account of my monsignor won't let me.

In the dining room Father Eudex sat down at the table and said grace. He helped himself to a chop, creamed new potatoes, pickled beets, jelly, and bread. He liked jelly. Monsignor passed the butter.

"That's supposed to be a tutti-frutti salad," Monsignor said, grimacing at his. "But she used green olives."

Father Eudex said nothing.

"I said she used green olives."

"I like green olives all right."

"I like green olives, but *not* in tutti-frutti salad."

Father Eudex replied by eating a green olive, but he knew it could not end there.

"Father," Monsignor said in a new tone. "How would you like to go away and study for a year?"

"Don't think I'd care for it, Monsignor. I'm not the type."

"You're no canonist, you mean?"

"That's one thing."

"Yes. Well, there are other things it might not hurt you to know. To be quite frank with you, Father, I think you need broadening."

"I guess so," Father Eudex said thickly.

"And still, with your tendencies . . . and with the universities honeycombed with Communists. No, that would never do. I think I meant seasoning, not broadening."

"Oh."

"No offense?"

"No offense."

Who would have thought a little thing like an olive could lead to all this, Father Eudex mused—who but himself, that is, for his association with Monsignor had shown him that anything could lead to everything. Monsignor was a master at making points. Nothing had changed since the day Father Eudex walked into the rectory saying he was the new assistant. Monsignor had evaded Father Eudex's hand in greeting, and a few days later, after he began to get the range, he delivered a lecture on the whole subject of handshaking. It was Middle West to shake hands, or South West, or West in any case, and it was not done where he came from, and—why had he ever come from where he came from? Not to be reduced to shaking hands, you could bet! Handshaking was worse than foot washing and unlike that pious practice there was nothing to support it. And from handshaking Monsignor might go into a general discussion of Father Eudex's failings. He used the open forum method, but he was the only speaker and there was never time enough for questions from the audience. Monsignor seized his examples at random from life. He saw Father Eudex coming out of his bedroom in pajama bottoms only and so told him about the dressing gown, its purpose, something of its history. He advised Father Eudex to barber his armpits, for it was being done all over now. He let Father Eudex see his bottle of cologne, "Steeple," special for clergymen, and said he should not be afraid of it. He suggested that Father Eudex shave his face oftener, too. He loaned him his Rogers Peet catalogue, which had sketches of clerical blades togged out in the latest, and prayed that he would stop going around looking like a rabbinical student.

He found Father Eudex reading *The Catholic Worker* one day and had not trusted him since. Father Eudex's conception of the priesthood was evangelical in the worst sense, barbaric, gross, foreign to the mind of the Church, which was one of two terms he used as sticks to beat him with. The other was taste. The air of the rectory was often heavy with The Mind of the Church and Taste.

Another thing. Father Eudex could not conduct a civil conversation. Monsignor doubted that Father Eudex could even think to himself with anything like agreement. Certainly any discussion with Father Eudex ended inevitably in argument or sighing. Sighing! Why didn't people talk up if they had anything to say? No, they'd rather sigh! Father, don't ever, ever sigh at me again!

Finally, Monsignor did not like Father Eudex's table manners. This came to a head one night when Monsignor, seeing his curate's plate empty and all the silverware at his place unused except for a single knife, fork, and spoon, exploded altogether, saying it had been on his mind for weeks, and then descending into the vernacular he declared that Father Eudex did not know the forks—now perhaps he could understand that! Meals, unless Monsignor had guests or other things to struggle with, were always occasions of instruction for Father Eudex, and sometimes of chastisement.

And now he knew the worst—if Monsignor was thinking of recommending him for a year of study, in a Sulpician seminary probably, to learn the forks. So this was what it meant to be a priest. *Come, follow me. Going forth, teach ye all nations. Heal the sick, raise the dead, cleanse the lepers, cast out devils.* Teach the class of people we get here? Teach Mr. Memmers? Teach Communists? Teach Monsignors? And where were the poor? The lepers of old? The lepers were in their colonies with nuns to nurse them. The poor were in their holes and would not come out. Mr. Memmers was in his bank, without cheer. The Communists were in their universities, awaiting a sign. And he was at table with Monsignor, and it was enough for the disciple to be as his master, but the housekeeper had used green olives.

Monsignor inquired, "Did you get your check today?"

Father Eudex, looking up, considered. "I got *a* check," he said.

"From the Rival people, I mean?"

"Yes."

"Good. Well, I think you might apply it on the car you're wanting. A decent car. That's a worthy cause." Monsignor noticed that he was not taking it well. "Not that I mean to dictate what you shall do with your little windfall, Father. It's just that I don't like to see you mortifying yourself with a Model A—and disgracing the Church."

"Yes," Father Eudex said, suffering.

"Yes. I dare say you don't see the danger, just as you didn't a while ago when I found you making a spectacle of yourself with Whalen. You just don't see the danger because you just don't think. Not to dwell on it, but I seem to remember some overshoes."

The overshoes! Monsignor referred to them as to the Fall. Last winter Father Eudex had given his overshoes to a freezing picket. It had got back to Monsignor and—good Lord, a man could have his sympathies, but he had no right clad in the cloth to endanger the prestige of the Church by siding in these wretched squabbles. Monsignor said he hated to think of all the evil done by people doing good! Had Father Eudex ever heard of the Albigensian heresy, or didn't the seminary teach that any more?

Father Eudex declined dessert. It was strawberry mousse.

"Delicious," Monsignor said. "I think I'll let her stay."

At that moment Father Eudex decided that he had nothing to lose. He placed his knife next to his fork on the plate, adjusted them this way and that until they seemed to work a combination in his mind, to spring a lock which in turn enabled him to speak out.

"Monsignor," he said. "I think I ought to tell you I don't intend to make use of that money. In fact—to show you how my mind works—I have even considered endorsing the check to the strikers' relief fund."

"So," Monsignor said calmly—years in the confessional had prepared him for anything.

"I'll admit I don't know whether I can in justice. And even if I could I don't know that I would. I don't know why . . . I guess hush money, no matter what you do with it, is lousy."

Monsignor regarded him with piercing baby blue eyes. "You'd find it pretty hard to prove, Father, that *any* money *in se* is . . . what you say it is. I would quarrel further with the definition 'hush money.' It seems to me nothing if not rash that you would presume to impugn the motive of the Rival Company in sending out these checks. You would seem to challenge the whole concept of good works—not that I am ignorant of the misuses to which money can be put." Monsignor, changing tack, tucked it all into a sigh. "Perhaps I'm just a simple soul, and it's enough for me to know personally some of the people in the Rival Company and to know them good people. Many of them Catholic . . ." A throb had crept into Monsignor's voice. He shut it off.

"I don't mean anything that subtle, Monsignor," Father Eudex said. "I'm just telling you, as my pastor, what I'm going to do with the check. Or what I'm not going to do with it. I don't know what I'm going to do with it. Maybe send it back."

Monsignor rose from the table, slightly smiling. "Very well, Father. But there's always the poor."

Monsignor took leave of Father Eudex with a laugh. Father Eudex felt it was supposed to fool him into thinking that nothing he had said would be used against him. It showed, rather, that Monsignor was not winded, that he had broken wild curates before, plenty of them, and that he would ride again.

Father Eudex sought the shade of the porch. He tried to read his office, but was drowsy. He got up for a glass of water. The saints in Ireland used to stand up to their necks in cold water, but not for drowsiness. When he came back to the porch a woman was ringing the doorbell. She looked like a customer for rosary beads.

"Hello," he said.

"I'm Mrs. Klein, Father, and I was wondering if you could help me out."

Father Eudex straightened a porch chair for her. "Please sit down."

"It's a German name, Father. Klein was German descent," she said, and added with a silly grin, "It ain't what you think, Father."

"I beg your pardon."

"Klein. Some think it's a Jew name. But they stole it from Klein."

Father Eudex decided to come back to that later. "You were wondering if I could help you?"

"Yes, Father. It's personal."

"Is it matter for confession?"

"Oh no, Father." He had made her blush.

"Then go ahead."

Mrs. Klein peered into the honeysuckle vines on either side of the porch for alien ears.

"No one can hear you, Mrs. Klein."

"Father—I'm just a poor widow," she said, and continued as though Father Eudex had just slandered the man. "Klein was awful good to me, Father."

"I'm sure he was."

"So good . . . and he went and left me all he had." She had begun to cry a little.

Father Eudex nodded gently. She was after something, probably not money, always the best bet—either that or a drunk in the family—but this one was not Irish. Perhaps just sympathy.

"I come to get your advice, Father. Klein always said, 'If you got a problem, Freda, see the priest.'"

"Do you need money?"

"I got more than I can use from the bakery."

"You have a bakery?"

Mrs. Klein nodded down the street. "That's my bakery. It was Klein's. The Purity."

"I go by there all the time," Father Eudex said, abandoning himself to her. He must stop trying to shape the conversation and let her work it out.

"Will you give me your advice, Father?" He felt that

she sensed his indifference and interpreted it as his way of
rejecting her. She either had no idea how little sense she
made or else supreme faith in him, as a priest, to see into
her heart.

"Just what is it you're after, Mrs. Klein?"

"He left me all he had, Father, but it's just laying in the
bank."

"And you want me to tell you what to do with it?"

"Yes, Father."

Father Eudex thought this might be interesting, certainly a change. He went back in his mind to the seminary
and the class in which they had considered the problem of
inheritances. Do we have any unfulfilled obligations? Are
we sure? . . . Are there any impedimenta? . . .

"Do you have any dependents, Mrs. Klein—any
children?"

"One boy, Father. I got him running the bakery. I pay
him good—too much, Father."

"Is 'too much' a living wage?"

"Yes, Father. He ain't got a family."

"A living wage is not too much," Father Eudex handed
down, sailing into the encyclical style without knowing it.

Mrs. Klein was smiling over having done something good
without knowing precisely what it was.

"How old is your son?"

"He's thirty-six, Father."

"Not married?"

"No, Father, but he's got him a girl." She giggled, and
Father Eudex, embarrassed, retied his shoe.

"But you don't care to make a will and leave this money
to your son in the usual way?"

"I guess I'll have to . . . if I die." Mrs. Klein was suddenly crushed and haunted, but whether by death or
charity, Father Eudex did not know.

"You don't have to, Mrs. Klein. There are many worthy
causes. And the worthiest is the cause of the poor. My
advice to you, if I understand your problem, is to give what
you have to someone who needs it."

Mrs. Klein just stared at him.

"You could even leave it to the archdiocese," he said,

completing the sentence to himself: but I don't recommend it in your case . . . with your tendencies. You look like an Indian giver to me.

But Mrs. Klein had got enough. "Huh!" she said, rising. "Well! You *are* a funny one!"

And then Father Eudex realized that she had come to him for a broker's tip. It was in the eyes. The hat. The dress. The shoes. "If you'd like to speak to the pastor," he said, "come back in the evening."

"You're a nice young man," Mrs. Klein said, rather bitter now and bent on getting away from him. "But I got to say this—you ain't much of a priest. And Klein said if I got a problem, see the priest—huh! You ain't much of a priest! What time's your boss come in?"

"In the evening," Father Eudex said. "Come any time in the evening."

Mrs. Klein was already down the steps and making for the street.

"You might try Mr. Memmers at the First National," Father Eudex called, actually trying to help her, but she must have thought it was just some more of his nonsense and did not reply.

After Mrs. Klein had disappeared Father Eudex went to his room. In the hallway upstairs Monsignor's voice, coming from the depths of the clerical nap, halted him.

"Who was it?"

"A woman," Father Eudex said. "A woman seeking good counsel."

He waited a moment to be questioned, but Monsignor was not awake enough to see anything wrong with that, and there came only a sigh and a shifting of weight that told Father Eudex he was simply turning over in bed.

Father Eudex walked into the bathroom. He took the Rival check from his pocket. He tore it into little squares. He let them flutter into the toilet. He pulled the chain— hard.

He went to his room and stood looking out the window at nothing. He could hear the others already giving an account of their stewardship, but could not judge them. I bought baseball uniforms for the school. I bought the nuns a new washing machine. I purchased a Mass kit for a Chinese missionary. I bought a set of matched irons. Mine helped pay for keeping my mother in a rest home upstate. I gave mine to the poor.

And you, Father?

Renner

Except for a contemporary placard or two, the place conspired to set me dreaming of the good old days I had never known. The furniture did it—the cloudy mirrors, the grandiose mahogany bar, the tables and chairs ornate with spools and scrollwork, the burnished brass coat hooks and cuspidors, all as shiny-ugly as the day they were made, and swillish brown paintings, inevitable subjects, fat tippling friars in cellars, velvet cavaliers elegantly eying sherry, the deadliest of still-life fruit, but no fishes on platters.

At a table across the room, Emil, the waiter, and two patrons finished a hand, talked about it, scraped the cards into a muddy deck. They spoke an aromatic mixture of English and German. Emil, a little spaniel of a man, fussed with his flapping sleeves and consoled the fat man whose king had not been good enough.

Renner, using both hands, elevated a glass of beer in momentary exposition, raised his eyes to heaven, and drank deeply. I wondered if, despite everything, he might still be fascinated by the Germans. I could think of no other reason for coming here.

I signaled Emil. He smiled too graciously, put down his cards, and came over to pick up our glasses, saying "Gentlemen." One of the cardplayers frowned at me for interrupting the game. He was the one we called the Entrepreneur. Renner had acquired his English abroad and reporters to him were journalists; the cardplayer, who might possibly be a salesman, had become an Entrepreneur.

When Emil brought our glasses back, quivering and amber, I became preoccupied with a button on my coat, escaping the gelatinous impact of his smile. I could sense Renner undergoing it. When Emil withdrew, Renner said, "He's not as simple as he pretends to be." This struck me as off-key to the point of being funny. And still it may have been that I had already recognized, without consciously acknowledging, something dimly sinister about Emil.

Renner dipped his glass at a bowl of fruit rotting on the wall. "It's too bad *der Fuehrer* couldn't paint a little. Another bad painter, we could have stood that." He began to speak in what I had come to know as his autobiographical tone. He appeared to listen to himself, skeptical, though he was accenting words and ideas, of the meaning in what he said, trying to account for himself on earth. "Anyway, my mother hired a sergeant major to discipline me when I was eight years old. The Austrian army was not the most formidable in the world, except of course at regimental balls, but she hoped he could do the job. He couldn't. I was not to have many such victories."

The idea of Renner the child died away when I looked at the man across the table from me. Renner had rusty hair, bristling abundantly, tufted eyebrows, an oddly handsome face with the depth and decision of a wood carving about it. When I looked again Renner the man was lost in our surroundings. I saw an album world: exaggerated bicycles and good-old-summertime girls, picnics and family reunions, mustachioed quartets, polished horses galloping through Budweiser advertisements, the heroes and adventures of Horatio Alger, the royal commerce of the day. The furniture reached boldly into the past and yanked these visions into being. I had only to step out the door to find everything changed back fifty years. Meanwhile the green walls, waiting to be smoked black, stood patiently around us.

"Because he could paint like that," Renner said, "my uncle became president of the Vienna Academy." I glanced needlessly at the pictures. Renner laughed shortly. "He had a patriarchal beard, however, which he used to clean his brushes on. His only attempt at eccentricity and it failed. In fact, it killed him—lead poisoning."

There was a fictitious feeling about sitting so casually with a man whose uncle had been president of an art academy. Renner himself had taught at the University of Vienna, had perhaps come into a little eminence of his own, but compared to his uncle he was small fry indeed. Achievement through violence or succession or cunning or even merit is common enough. But president of an academy of art—now there was an inscrutable honor, beyond accounting for, like being an archbishop (except in Italy), only more so.

A dark man in tweeds came in. Emil threw down his cards, rushed to meet him, and the two left at the table turned slowly to see. First disappointed, then a little disgusted, they turned up Emil's cards on the table.

"My good friend, Mr. Ross," Emil purred. Mr. Ross extended his hand and they stood there shaking, smiling at each other. Mr. Ross finally got around to saying he came in for a glass. Emil went behind the bar and took down a bottle of brandy. Emil was still oppressing Mr. Ross with his smile, but Mr. Ross seemed to think it no more than right or less than real.

"Well, Renner," I said. Renner, who had been watching them, began talking again—against his will, I thought, but anxious to get Emil and Mr. Ross out of our minds.

"At the beginning of the last war—this was in Innsbruck —we had a geometry teacher, very droll. He'd get furious and throw the squares and triangles at the pupils. He also rode a horse, as if in battle, to school. He would say, 'Miller, what color should I make this line?'—some line in geometry; he'd be standing at the blackboard. 'Red,' Miller would answer. 'Why red, Miller?' You see the pupils knew what to say, I among them. 'Red for the blood of the Serbs, Herr Professor.' 'Very good, Miller! And this line, Scheutzer?' 'Yellow—for the enemy.' 'Very good!' You know," Renner said, "the man of action," and was silent.

"I know."

"Delightful task," as one of the cheery English poets says, "to rear the tender thought, to teach the young idea how to shoot."

I almost added that the geometry teacher, if living, must be cherished by the Fatherland today, but I thought better of it: such men are everywhere, never without a country.

Emil was begging Mr. Ross to stay for a bite to eat. At first Mr. Ross refused and then, overcome by the fervor of Emil's invitation, he said he would look at the menu.

"You won't need to look today, Mr. Ross." Emil rubbed his hands in polite ecstasy, became intent, his eyes glazed, as though savoring some impossible dream. "The pike," he said, "is delicious." But rare Mr. Ross was reluctant to have pike. "Well, then!" Emil said, pretending outrage; he handed Mr. Ross his fate in the menu. He folded his arms and waited scornfully.

Immediately Mr. Ross proclaimed: "Chicken livers and mushrooms."

Emil showed a suffering cheerfulness, shaking his head, the good loser. Plainly Mr. Ross had divined chicken livers and mushrooms against all Emil's efforts to keep them in the kitchen for himself. "Ah, they're very excellent today, Mr. Ross."

All this playing at old world *délicatesse* seemed to annoy Renner too much. Slowly he began to ramble, his eyes fixed on Emil, as though it were all there to be read in his face. "You wouldn't think a little stenographer would remember what you said for ten years back and write it down every night—and the day they sent for you (bring two suits of underclothes and a roll of toilet paper; we'll do the rest) you'd hear it all then, also recordings they'd made of your telephone conversations . . . because there were little telephone operators like the little stenographer. . . ." Renner stopped speaking when Emil went into the kitchen, as if the inspiration to continue were gone with Emil.

"Is Mr. Ross Jewish?" I asked.

Renner nodded indistinctly.

On occasion I had wondered whether Renner was Jewish, always halfheartedly, so that I forgot what I was wondering about, and it would be a while before I wondered again. His being a refugee proved nothing so specific or simple as that: his species, spiritually speaking, tends to make itself at home in exile.

Emil came out of the kitchen with bread, butter, and a dish of beets.

"I don't want those," Mr. Ross said—cruelly, it seemed to me, for Emil dearly wanted him to have them. Then it occurred to me that it was part of Mr. Ross's grand manner. He had considered the saving to Emil and his own

loss in waving aside the bread, butter, and beets. It had
been a telling act and there could be no turning back. Emil
propitiated him with a devout and carefully uncomprehend-
ing look, such as he must have fancied appropriate to
menials like himself and soothing to men of business like
Mr. Ross.

The Entrepreneur leaned forward and spoke passionately
in German to the fat one, who agreed with him, nodding
and grunting.

"Now what?" I asked Renner.

Renner listened further before venturing a translation.
"Well," he said finally, as though I would not be getting
the whole story. "A certain man is a good bookkeeper, but
not a good businessman."

"But the Entrepreneur is?"

"He is." Renner began to deliberate in a familiar voice,
not his own. "It's all right, this tobacco. But I"—a very
capital I—"I would never pay twenty-five cents. I would pay,
say, twenty." He struck a match, touched the flame to his
pipe, looked shrewd, and blew out a mouthful of smoke to
close the deal. It was the voice of the superintendent
where we both worked, and it was Renner's theory, to
which I subscribed, that the super haggled about everything
because secretly he yearned to be a purchasing agent.

Renner watched the cardplayers. "The Entrepreneur has
a very expressive head, too." I could see what Renner
meant. Seen, as now, from the rear, the Entrepreneur's
head was most expressive. I had noticed his face before;
it was gross and uninteresting.

"In fact," Renner said, "they are almost identical."

"What?"

"Their heads *par derrière*, the Entrepreneur's and the
super's. I think it's mostly in the ears. They both have
histrionic ears. Seismographic instruments. See. The Entrepreneur needs no face or voice or hands. His ears tell all."

The back of the Entrepreneur's head grimaced, his ears
blushed, and his hand slapped a losing card on the table.
He snarled something in German.

"You see!" Renner said. "Just like the super—*dynamic!*"

When Renner used a word like "dynamic" he thought he was very American.

I took out my pipe. Renner shoved the package of to-bacco across the table. "Stalin imports tobacco from this country, did you know? No one else in Russia may." A re-vealing sidelight, it seemed to me, and I hoped Renner's source was obscure, if not reliable. "Edgeworth," Renner said. "Stalin smokes only Edgeworth."

"Think of the dilemma Stalin's endorsement must con-stitute for the Edgeworth company," I reflected. "One fac-tion wants to launch the product as the choice of dictators."

Renner took up the idea. "Another faction doggedly holds out for the common man."

"Finally," I said, slightly excited, "a futile attempt (by visionaries in the advertising department) to square the circle."

"We can't all be dictators," Renner broke in like a radio announcer, "but we can all——"

"Exactly."

A stocky man plodded out of the washroom. The card-players hardly noticed him. I could not help thinking of him in terms of *deus ex machina*, for we had not seen him before and we had been in the place too long. He stood in the middle of the floor, a crumpled, somewhat parlia-mentary figure, and said:

"If I was sober . . ."

Then, accounting for his long exile in the washroom, he dislodged from his coat pocket a newspaper, folded edi-torial page out, and threw it with a sigh across the mahog-any bar. He sat down in the empty fourth chair at the card table. This, too, seemed to be foreordained. The fat one dealt him in without comment. Emil laid down his cards, disappeared into the kitchen, and returned with a cup of something, probably black coffee. The stocky man received it silently, his just due, and drank. He put the cup, wobbling, down and said:

"If I was sober . . ."

"Irish," I said.

"An age-old alliance," Renner said. "The Irish and the Germans."

There was, in fact, a rough unity about them. The fat one and the Entrepreneur thrust themselves in and seemed to maintain their positions with a forcefulness suggesting fear. Emil, with whom cordiality was a method, never granted a more confidential glance to one than to another, and by the very falsity of his servility distinguished himself as a strong character. The stocky Irishman, who had pleasant puffy eyes and vigorous wattles, loomed up as a most accomplished fact. He was closer to the furniture than the others, a druid. While the fat one and the Entrepreneur experienced mortal joy and sorrow, according to their luck at cards, and Emil dealt nervously in camaraderie, the Irishman was satisfied to be present and one with the universe. One thing was sure: they all *belonged*.

Emil sacrificed his place at the card table and plied efficiently among his patrons. He brought us beer, the cardplayers drinks and matches, and Mr. Ross delicacies and homage. When Emil came by the cardplayers' table, I heard them urge him to get through with the carriage trade. That could mean only Mr. Ross, for he was being smiled and grunted at among them. They could tell that he had a romantic concept of the place. It was celebrated now and then by broken book reviewers as the erstwhile hearth of the nation's literary great. Perhaps poor, tweedy Mr. Ross was drunk with longing for a renaissance in letters and took the cardplayers for poets. They, I suspected, were all worried about how Mr. Ross made his money where he'd just come from and aggravated to think (the Jews got all the money!) he'd be going back to make more when he left. It seemed to pain Renner that Mr. Ross could confide in Emil and permit him clucking around his table.

Renner breathed over his empty glass and resumed his autobiography. Some middle chapters seemed to be missing, for we were in New York in 1939. "Some employment agencies had signs saying sixteen or seventeen dishwashers wanted. I just stood in the doorway and the agent waved his hand—No! Others, too; one look at me and—No! They're very good, they know their business, the agents."

"What about teaching?"

"*Ja*, sure. That was interesting, too. 'Of course you've

taught for years at the University of Vienna' "—Renner reproduced a stilted voice and I knew we were at an interview he must have had—" 'but surely you must know that what counts in this country is a degree from Columbia, Harvard, or here, the *only* schools for political science. I thought *everyone* knew that. I suggest you try one of the smaller schools.'

"So I tried one of the smaller plants. I went to a teachers' agency and eventually entered into correspondence with a Midwestern college. 'It is true' "—here was another, more nasal voice—" 'that there is an opening on our staff for a qualified man in your field, but it is true also that it will remain vacant till doomsday before we appoint a tobacco addict, especially one constrained to advertise that sorry fact.' A veiled reference," Renner laughed, "to the pipe in the snapshot I sent."

"American Gothic," I said.

"Just as well," he said. "I was through with teaching when I left Europe. Too much guilt connected with it. Although clergymen and educators are not so influential as might be supposed from pulpits and commencement addresses, and the real influences are the grocer, the alderman, the radio comedian (and of course the men who pay them), still that's pretty shabby exoneration. . . ."

I noticed that Renner had become angry and disheveled. Poor Renner! It was his wife's lament that nothing roused him. She had made herself an enemy to the Heimwehr in Vienna and been forced to leave Austria long before the Nazis arrived, bringing their own brand of fascism to the extermination of the local product. Renner had stayed on, however, reading in the cafés (he'd lost out at the University through his wife's activities) and thinking nothing could happen to him—until everything did. His wife, in judging him lethargic, was wrong in the way such vigilant people can never detect. Renner, I believe, was only insensitive to political events, to the eternal traffic jams of empires, and felt it was hardly his fault that he lived when and where he did in time and space. If he had been a boy, he would not have believed he might someday be President, nor even have wished it.

I could understand from this what he meant when he said, in one of his extravagant statements, that he loved horses and foxes and could not forgive the English for what they do to both. Those were the symbols he chose through which to make himself known (at least to me), although it was by no means certain that they were only symbols to him. When he spoke of foxes and horses it was with no shade of poetry or whimsey or condescension. His face became intense and I could easily imagine him in a kind of restricted paradise: just foxes, horses, himself, and a lot of Rousseau vegetation. Of all the animals, he said, only the horse lives in a state of uninterrupted insanity.

Renner took a large swallow from his glass and set it down with a noise. "For nineteen hundred years they've been doing that."

"Who? What?"

"Plato's learned men. Capitulating. I say nineteen hundred years, though it's longer, because Christ cut the ground from under them—the Scribes and Pharisees of old. He gave us a new law. Martyrdom, indecent as it sounds to our itching ears, is not supposed to be too much to suffer for it."

"Speak for yourself, Renner," I said.

"Aren't you a Christian?"

"Of course. But my idea of Christianity is the community fund, doing good, and brisk mottoes on the wall."

"Copulating with circumstance," Renner said.

I looked at the cardplayers and there they were, overwhelming aspects of human endeavor: the fat one and the Entrepreneur throwing themselves soulfully into their best cards, the table dumbly standing for it, the Irishman piled up warmly and lifelessly, except for his fingers flicking the cards and his eyes which blinked occasionally, keeping watch over the body. I caught Emil's eye, which he proceeded to twinkle at me, and he came over for our glasses. Renner kept his eyes down and so I was stuck with meeting Emil's smile. I could not bring myself to return it. I told him the beer was good, very—when he waited for more—very good beer. When he came from the bar with our glasses filled he explained in detail how the beer came to be so good and did his smile until I felt positively damp from it.

❧ "A little tragedy took place in our department this afternoon," Renner said, after Emil had gone. "Victoria Marzak versus the super"—for whom Renner indicated the Entrepreneur; I was confused until I remembered their heads were alike. "It was three acts, beginning with Victoria giving the super hell because working conditions are so bad in the stock rooms (which they are). She delivered a nice little declaration of independence. I thought the day had finally arrived. The workers of the world were about to throw off their chains and forget their social security numbers. The super said nothing in this act.

"In the next, however, he went into action. He surpassed Victoria in both wrath and righteousness. His thesis, as much of it as I could understand, was that Victoria and the girls could not expect better conditions—for the duration. Victoria said it was the first she'd heard of our being a war plant. The super mentioned our ashtrays and picture frames, and said she ought to feel ashamed of herself, always complaining, when there were boys dying in foxholes —yes, boys who needed our products. Ashtrays in foxholes! I thought he was laying it on too thick at this point, even for him, and I did a foolish thing. We won't go into that now, as it might obscure the larger meaning of the tragedy.

"Act Three was classic, revealing the history of human progress, or the effects of original sin (reason darkened), depending on your taste in terminology. The super introduced Victoria to the supernatural element, which in our department goes by the name of Pressure From Above. He invoked Pressure as the first cause of all conditions, including working. In short, the less said about conditions the better. Victoria wilted. But Pressure, besides being a just and jealous god, is merciful. The super forgave her trespasses, said he was working on a raise for her, and she went back to her job (under the same conditions), beating her sizable breast and crying *mea culpa* for having inveighed against them—conditions, that is—as things sacred to Pressure. Curtain."

Renner rubbed his eyes and gazed past me. Mr. Ross

had risen from the chicken livers and mushrooms. Emil stacked the dishes for removal.

"I want to pay you for everything," Mr. Ross said, meaning, I presumed, the bread, butter, and beets. The card-players looked at each other wisely at this, as though the law had thus been fulfilled.

"In case you are wondering," Renner continued, "Victoria represents suffering humanity suffering as it was in the beginning, is now, and ever shall be, world without end."

"Amen," I said.

Renner's voice cracked and he began again. "How did the Austrian Socialists, the best organized working-class group in history and pacifists to boot, reconcile themselves to the war in 1914?"

"No doubt they organized committees," I said, "or took the ever-lovin' long view."

"Worse. Dressed in the Emperor's uniforms and crammed in boxcars ordinarily reserved for cattle, they rode off shouting—imagine—'Down with the Czar and Imperialism!'"

"A distinction to make a theologian blush," I said. "But tell me, what was this foolish thing you did in the second act?"

"I stood up to the super and told him a few things, mostly concerning the rights and dignity of man."

I considered the implications of this for a moment. "Then, as we say, you are no longer with the company?"

"Yes."

"You were fired?"

"Yes. Insubordination."

Emil was telling Mr. Ross how much everything was. Mr. Ross pulled out a couple of bills and pressed them blindly into Emil's hand.

"And the rest is for the house," Mr. Ross said. The card-players sniffed at each other and shared their disgust. Emil thanked Mr. Ross from the bottom of his heart, shook his hand, put it down, and took it up for a final shaking.

At the door Mr. Ross turned smartly and waved a large farewell which seemed to include Renner and me and the poets playing pinochle. Then he vanished into the street.

"Good-by, Mr. Ross," Emil said plaintively, as if to his memory. Emil went to the card table, sat down, and fooled with his sleeves. The Entrepreneur, dealing, jerked his head at the door, snarled something in German, and went on dealing. The fat one nodded and belched lightly. The Irishman closed his eyes in a long blink. Emil grinned at his cards.

"That was Mr. Ross," he said.

"So that was Mr. Ross," the Entrepreneur said, attempting Yiddish dialect.

Abruptly Renner stood up, jolting our table sharply, his face all swollen and red, and started across the floor. Before I could get up and interfere, he came to a wavering halt. Looking at him were four surprised faces and there seemed to be nothing about them familiar or hateful to Renner. Evidently he was bewildered to find no super: he had seen his head a moment before. He gave me an ashamed look which was not without resentment. Then he walked back to our table, stuck his pipe, which was lying there, in his pocket, threw down some money, and went out the door.

The Valiant Woman

They had come to the dessert in a dinner that was a shambles. "Well, John," Father Nulty said, turning away from Mrs. Stoner and to Father Firman, long gone silent at his own table. "You've got the bishop coming for confirmations next week."

"Yes," Mrs. Stoner cut in, "and for dinner. And if he don't eat any more than he did last year——"

Father Firman, in a rare moment, faced it. "Mrs. Stoner, the bishop is not well. You know that."

"And after I fixed that fine dinner and all." Mrs. Stoner pouted in Father Nulty's direction.

"I wouldn't feel bad about it, Mrs. Stoner," Father Nulty said. "He never eats much anywhere."

"It's funny. And that new Mrs. Allers said he ate just fine when he was there," Mrs. Stoner argued, and then spit out, "but she's a damned liar!"

Father Nulty, unsettled but trying not to show it, said, "Who's Mrs. Allers?"

"She's at Holy Cross," Mrs. Stoner said.

"She's the housekeeper," Father Firman added, thinking Mrs. Stoner made it sound as though Mrs. Allers were the pastor there.

"I swear I don't know what to do about the dinner this year," Mrs. Stoner said.

Father Firman moaned. "Just do as you've always done, Mrs. Stoner."

"Huh! And have it all to throw out! Is that any way to do?"

"Is there any dessert?" Father Firman asked coldly.

Mrs. Stoner leaped up from the table and bolted into the kitchen, mumbling. She came back with a birthday cake. She plunged it in the center of the table. She found a big wooden match in her apron pocket and thrust it at Father Firman.

"I don't like this bishop," she said. "I never did. And the way he went and cut poor Ellen Kennedy out of Father Doolin's will!"

She went back into the kitchen.

"Didn't they talk a lot of filth about Doolin and the housekeeper?" Father Nulty asked.

"I should think they did," Father Firman said. "All because he took her to the movies on Sunday night. After he died and the bishop cut her out of the will, though I hear he gives her a pension privately, they talked about the bishop."

"I don't like this bishop at all," Mrs. Stoner said, appearing with a cake knife. "Bishop Doran—there was the man!"

"We know," Father Firman said. "All man and all priest."

"He did know real estate," Father Nulty said.

Father Firman struck the match.

"Not on the chair!" Mrs. Stoner cried, too late.

Father Firman set the candle burning—it was suspiciously large and yellow, like a blessed one, but he could not be sure. They watched the fluttering flame.

"I'm forgetting the lights!" Mrs. Stoner said, and got up to turn them off. She went into the kitchen again.

The priests had a moment of silence in the candlelight.

"Happy birthday, John," Father Nulty said softly. "Is it fifty-nine you are?"

"As if you didn't know, Frank," Father Firman said, "and you the same but one."

Father Nulty smiled, the old gold of his incisors shining in the flickering light, his collar whiter in the dark, and raised his glass of water, which would have been wine or better in the bygone days, and toasted Father Firman.

"Many of 'em, John."

"Blow it out," Mrs. Stoner said, returning to the room. She waited by the light switch for Father Firman to blow out the candle.

Mrs. Stoner, who ate no desserts, began to clear the dishes into the kitchen, and the priests, finishing their cake and coffee in a hurry, went to sit in the study.

Father Nulty offered a cigar.

"John?"

"My ulcers, Frank."

"Ah, well, you're better off." Father Nulty lit the cigar and crossed his long black legs. "Fish Frawley has got him a Filipino, John. Did you hear?"

Father Firman leaned forward, interested. "He got rid of the woman he had?"

"He did. It seems she snooped."

"Snooped, eh?"

"She did. And gossiped. Fish introduced two town boys to her, said, 'Would you think these boys were my nephews?' That's all, and the next week the paper had it that his two nephews were visiting him from Erie. After that, he let her believe he was going East to see his parents, though both are dead. The paper carried the story. Fish returned and made a sermon out of it. Then he got the Filipino."

Father Firman squirmed with pleasure in his chair. "That's like Fish, Frank. He can do that." He stared at the tips of his fingers bleakly. "You could never get a Filipino to come to a place like this."

"Probably not," Father Nulty said. "Fish is pretty close to Minneapolis. Ah, say, do you remember the trick he played on us all in Marmion Hall?"

"That I'll not forget!" Father Firman's eyes remembered. "Getting up New Year's morning and finding the toilet seats all painted!"

"*Happy Circumcision!* Hah!" Father Nulty had a coughing fit.

When he had got himself together again, a mosquito came and sat on his wrist. He watched it a moment before bringing his heavy hand down. He raised his hand slowly, viewed the dead mosquito, and sent it spinning with a plunk of his middle finger.

"Only the female bites," he said.

"I didn't know that," Father Firman said.

"Ah, yes . . ."

Mrs. Stoner entered the study and sat down with some sewing—Father Firman's black socks.

She smiled pleasantly at Father Nulty. "And what do you think of the atom bomb, Father?"

"Not much," Father Nulty said.

Mrs. Stoner had stopped smiling. Father Firman yawned.

Mrs. Stoner served up another: "Did you read about this communist convert, Father?"

"He's been in the Church before," Father Nulty said, "and so it's not a conversion, Mrs. Stoner."

"No? Well, I already got him down on my list of Monsignor's converts."

"It's better than a conversion, Mrs. Stoner, for there is more rejoicing in heaven over the return of . . . uh, he that was lost, Mrs. Stoner, is found."

"And that congresswoman, Father?"

"Yes. A convert—she."

"And Henry Ford's grandson, Father. I got him down."

"Yes, to be sure."

Father Firman yawned, this time audibly, and held his jaw.

"But he's one only by marriage, Father," Mrs. Stoner said. "I always say you got to watch those kind."

"Indeed you do, but a convert nonetheless, Mrs. Stoner. Remember, Cardinal Newman himself was one."

Mrs. Stoner was unimpressed. "I see where Henry Ford's making steering wheels out of soybeans, Father."

"I didn't see that."

"I read it in the *Reader's Digest* or some place."

"Yes, well . . ." Father Nulty rose and held his hand out to Father Firman. "John," he said. "It's been good."

"I heard Hirohito's next," Mrs. Stoner said, returning to converts.

"Let's wait and see, Mrs. Stoner," Father Nulty said.

The priests walked to the door.

"You know where I live, John."

"Yes. Come again, Frank. Good night."

Father Firman watched Father Nulty go down the walk to his car at the curb. He hooked the screen door and turned off the porch light. He hesitated at the foot of the stairs, suddenly moved to go to bed. But he went back into the study.

"Phew!" Mrs. Stoner said. "I thought he'd never go. Here it is after eight o'clock."

Father Firman sat down in his rocking chair. "I don't see him often," he said.

"I give up!" Mrs. Stoner exclaimed, flinging the holey socks upon the horsehair sofa. "I'd swear you had a nail in your shoe."

"I told you I looked."

"Well, you ought to look again. And cut your toenails, why don't you? Haven't I got enough to do?"

Father Firman scratched in his coat pocket for a pill, found one, swallowed it. He let his head sink back against the chair and closed his eyes. He could hear her moving about the room, making the preparations; and how he knew them—the fumbling in the drawer for a pencil with a point, the rip of the page from his daily calendar, and finally the leg of the card table sliding up against his leg.

He opened his eyes. She yanked the floor lamp alongside the table, setting the bead fringe tinkling on the shade, and pulled up her chair on the other side. She sat down and smiled at him for the first time that day. Now she was happy.

She swept up the cards and began to shuffle with the abandoned virtuosity of an old river-boat gambler, standing them on end, fanning them out, whirling them through her fingers, dancing them halfway up her arms, cracking the whip over them. At last they lay before him tamed into a neat deck.

"Cut?"

"Go ahead," he said. She liked to go first.

She gave him her faint, avenging smile and drew a card, cast it aside for another which he thought must be an ace from the way she clutched it face down.

She was getting all the cards, as usual, and would have been invincible if she had possessed his restraint and if her cunning had been of a higher order. He knew a few things about leading and lying back that she would never learn. Her strategy was attack, forever attack, with one baffling departure: she might sacrifice certain tricks as expendable if only she could have the last ones, the heartbreaking ones, if she could slap them down one after another, shatteringly.

She played for blood, no bones about it, but for her there was no other way; it was her nature, as it was the lion's, and for this reason he found her ferocity pardonable, more a defect of the flesh, venial, while his own trouble was all in the will, mortal. He did not sweat and pray over each card as she must, but he did keep an eye out for reneging and demanded a cut now and then just to aggravate her, and he was always secretly hoping for aces.

With one card left in her hand, the telltale trick coming next, she delayed playing it, showing him first the smile, the preview of defeat. She laid it on the table—so! She held one more trump than he had reasoned possible. Had she palmed it from somewhere? No, she would not go that far; that would not be fair, was worse than reneging, which so easily and often happened accidentally, and she believed in being fair. Besides he had been watching her.

God smote the vines with hail, the sycamore trees with frost, and offered up the flocks to the lightning—but Mrs. Stoner! What a cross Father Firman had from God in Mrs. Stoner! There were other housekeepers as bad, no doubt, walking the rectories of the world, yes, but . . . yes. He could name one and maybe two priests who were worse off. One, maybe two. Cronin. His scraggly blonde of sixty—take her, with her everlasting banging on the grand piano, the gift of the pastor; her proud talk about the goiter operation at the Mayo Brothers', also a gift; her honking the parish Buick at passing strange priests because they were all in the game together. She was worse. She was something to keep the home fires burning. Yes sir. And Cronin said she was not a bad person really, but what was he? He was quite a freak himself.

For that matter, could anyone say that Mrs. Stoner was a bad person? No. He could not say it himself, and he was no freak. She had her points, Mrs. Stoner. She was clean. And though she cooked poorly, could not play the organ, would not take up the collection in an emergency, and went to card parties, and told all—even so, she was clean. She washed everything. Sometimes her underwear hung down beneath her dress like a paratrooper's pants, but it and everything she touched was clean. She washed constantly. She was clean.

She had her other points, to be sure—her faults, you might say. She snooped—no mistake about it—but it was not snooping for snooping's sake; she had a reason. She did other things, always with a reason. She overcharged on rosaries and prayer books, but that was for the sake of the poor. She censored the pamphlet rack, but that was to prevent scandal. She pried into the baptismal and matrimonial records, but there was no other way if Father was out, and in this way she had once uncovered a bastard and flushed him out of the rectory, but that was the perverted decency of the times. She held her nose over bad marriages in the presence of the victims, but that was her sorrow and came from having her husband buried in a mine. And he had caught her telling a bewildered young couple that there was only one good reason for their wanting to enter into a mixed marriage—the child had to have a name, and that—that was what?

She hid his books, kept him from smoking, picked his friends (usually the pastors of her colleagues), bawled out people for calling after dark, had no humor, except at cards, and then it was grim, very grim, and she sat hatchet-faced every morning at Mass. But she went to Mass, which was all that kept the church from being empty some mornings. She did annoying things all day long. She said annoying things into the night. She said she had given him the best years of her life. Had she? Perhaps—for the miner had her only a year. It was too bad, sinfully bad, when he thought of it like that. But all talk of best years and life was nonsense. He had to consider the heart of the matter, the essence. The essence was that housekeepers were hard to get, harder to get than ushers, than willing workers, than organists, than secretaries—yes, harder to get than assistants or vocations.

And she was a *saver*—saved money, saved electricity, saved string, bags, sugar, saved—him. That's what she did.

That's what she said she did, and she was right, in a way. In a way, she was usually right. In fact, she was always right—in a way. And you could never get a Filipino to come way out here and live. Not a young one anyway, and he had never seen an old one. Not a Filipino. They liked to dress up and live.

Should he let it drop about Fish having one, just to throw a scare into her, let her know he was doing some thinking? No. It would be a perfect cue for the one about a man needing a woman to look after him. He was not up to that again, not tonight.

Now she was doing what she liked most of all. She was making a grand slam, playing it out card for card, though it was in the bag, prolonging what would have been cut short out of mercy in gentle company. Father Firman knew the agony of losing.

She slashed down the last card, a miserable deuce trump, and did in the hapless king of hearts he had been saving.

"Skunked you!"

She was awful in victory. Here was the bitter end of their long day together, the final murderous hour in which all they wanted to say—all he wouldn't and all she couldn't— came out in the cards. Whoever won at honeymoon won the day, slept on the other's scalp, and God alone had to help the loser.

"We've been at it long enough, Mrs. Stoner," he said, seeing her assembling the cards for another round.

"Had enough, huh!"

Father Firman grumbled something.

"No?"

"Yes."

She pulled the table away and left it against the wall for the next time. She went out of the study carrying the socks, content and clucking. He closed his eyes after her and began to get under way in the rocking chair, the nightly trip to nowhere. He could hear her brewing a cup of tea in the kitchen and conversing with the cat. She made her way up the stairs, carrying the tea, followed by the cat, purring.

He waited, rocking out to sea, until she would be sure to be through in the bathroom. Then he got up and locked the front door (she looked after the back door) and loosened his collar going upstairs.

In the bathroom he mixed a glass of antiseptic, always afraid of pyorrhea, and gargled to ward off pharyngitis.

When he turned on the light in his room, the moths and beetles began to batter against the screens, the lighter insects humming. . . .

Yes, and she had the guest room. How did she come to get that? Why wasn't she in the back room, in her proper place? He knew, if he cared to remember. The screen in the back room—it let in mosquitoes, and if it didn't do that she'd love to sleep back there, Father, looking out at the steeple and the blessed cross on top, Father, if it just weren't for the screen, Father. Very well, Mrs. Stoner, I'll get it fixed or fix it myself. Oh, could you now, Father? I could, Mrs. Stoner, and I will. In the meantime you take the guest room. Yes, Father, and thank you, Father, the house ringing with amenities then. Years ago, all that. She was a pie-faced girl then, not really a girl perhaps, but not too old to marry again. But she never had. In fact, he could not remember that she had even tried for a husband since coming to the rectory, but, of course, he could be wrong, not knowing how they went about it. God! God save us! Had she got her wires crossed and mistaken him all these years for *that*? *That!* Him! Suffering God! No. That was going too far. That was getting morbid. No. He must not think of that again, ever. No.

But just the same she had got the guest room and she had it yet. Well, did it matter? Nobody ever came to see him any more, nobody to stay overnight anyway, nobody to stay very long . . . not any more. He knew how they laughed at him. He had heard Frank humming all right— before he saw how serious and sad the situation was and took pity—humming, "Wedding Bells Are Breaking Up That Old Gang of Mine." But then they'd always laughed at him for something—for not being an athlete, for wearing glasses, for having kidney trouble . . . and mail coming addressed to Rev. and Mrs. Stoner.

Removing his shirt, he bent over the table to read the volume left open from last night. He read, translating easily, "Eisdem licet cum illis . . . Clerics are allowed to reside only with women about whom there can be no suspicion, either because of a natural bond (as mother, sister, aunt) or of advanced age, combined in both cases with good repute."

Last night he had read it, and many nights before, each time as though this time to find what was missing, to find what obviously was not in the paragraph, his problem considered, a way out. She was not mother, not sister, not aunt, and *advanced age* was a relative term (why, she was younger than he was) and so, eureka, she did not meet the letter of the law—but, alas, how she fulfilled the spirit! And besides it would be a slimy way of handling it after all her years of service. He could not afford to pension her off, either.

He slammed the book shut. He slapped himself fiercely on the back, missing the wily mosquito, and whirled to find it. He took a magazine and folded it into a swatter. Then he saw it—oh, the preternatural cunning of it!—poised in the beard of St. Joseph on the bookcase. He could not hit it there. He teased it away, wanting it to light on the wall, but it knew his thoughts and flew high away. He swung wildly, hoping to stun it, missed, swung back, catching St. Joseph across the neck. The statue fell to the floor and broke.

Mrs. Stoner was panting in the hall outside his door.

"What is it?"

"Mosquitoes!"

"What is it, Father? Are you hurt?"

"Mosquitoes—damn it! And only the female bites!"

Mrs. Stoner, after a moment, said, "Shame on you, Father. She needs the blood for her eggs."

He dropped the magazine and lunged at the mosquito with his bare hand.

She went back to her room, saying, "Pshaw, I thought it was burglars murdering you in your bed."

He lunged again.

The Eye

All them that dropped in at Bullen's last night was talking about the terrible accident that almost happened to Clara Beck—that's Clyde Bullen's best girl. I am in complete charge of the pool tables and cigar counter, including the punchboards, but I am not at my regular spot in front, on account of Clyde has got a hot game of rotation going at the new table, and I am the only one he will leave chalk his cue. While I am chalking it and collecting for games and racking the balls I am hearing from everybody how Clara got pulled out of the river by Sleep Bailey.

He is not one of the boys, Sleep, but just a nigger that's deef and lives over in jigtown somewhere and plays the piano for dances at the Louisiana Social Parlor. They say he can't hear nothing but music. Spends the day loafing and fishing. He's fishing—is the story—when he seed Clara in the river below the Ludlow road bridge, and he swum out and saved her. Had to knock her out to do it, she put up such a fight. Anyways he saved her from drownding. That was the story everybody was telling.

Clyde has got the idee of taking up a collection for Sleep, as it was a brave deed he done and he don't have nothing to his name but a tub of fishing worms. On the other hand, he don't need nothing, being a nigger, not needing nothing. But Clara is Clyde's girl and it is Clyde's idee and so it is going over pretty big as most of the boys is trying to stay in with Clyde and the rest is owing him money and can't help themselves. I chipped in two bits myself.

Clyde is just fixing to shoot when Skeeter Bird comes in and says, "Little cold for swimming, ain't it, Clyde?"

It upsets Clyde and he has to line up the thirteen ball again. I remember it is the thirteen 'cause they ain't nobody round here that's got the eye Clyde has got for them big balls and that thirteen is his special favor-ite, says it's lucky—it and the nine. I tell you this on account of

Clyde misses his shot. Looked to me and anybody else that knowed Clyde's game that what Skeeter said upset his aim.

"What's eating you?" Clyde says to Skeeter, plenty riled. I can see he don't feel so bad about the thirteen getting away as he might of, as he has left it sewed up for Ace Haskins, that claims he once took a game from the great Ralph Greenleaf. "You got something to say?" Clyde says.

"No," Skeeter says, "only——"

"Only what?" Clyde wants to know.

"Only that Bailey nigger got hisself scratched up nice, Clyde."

"So I am taking up a little collection for him," Clyde says. "Pass the plate to Brother Bird, boys."

But Skeeter, he don't move a finger, just says, "Clara got banged up some, too, Clyde. Nigger must of socked her good."

None of us knowed what Skeeter was getting at, except maybe Clyde, that once took a course in mind reading, but we don't like it. And Clyde, I can tell, don't like it. The cue stick is shaking a little in his hand like he wants to use it on Skeeter and he don't shoot right away. He straightens up and says, "Well, he hadda keep her from strangling him while he was rescuing her, didn't he? It was for her own good."

"Yeah, guess so," Skeeter says. "But they both looked like they been in a mean scrap."

"That so?" Clyde says. "Was you there?"

"No, but I heard," Skeeter says.

"You heard," Clyde says. He gets ready to drop the fifteen.

"Yeah," Skeeter says. "You know, Clyde, that Bailey nigger is a funny nigger."

"How's that?" Clyde says, watching Skeeter close. "What's wrong with him?" Clyde holds up his shot and looks right at Skeeter. "Come on, out with it."

"Oh, I don't know as they's a lot wrong with him," Skeeter says. "I guess he's all right. Lazy damn nigger is all. Won't keep a job—just wants to play on the piano and fish."

"Never would of rescued Clara if he didn't," Clyde says. "And besides what kind of job you holding down?"

Now that gets Skeeter where it hurts on account of he don't work hisself, unless you call selling rubbers work or peddling art studies work. Yeah, that's what he calls them. Art studies. Shows a girl that ain't got no clothes on, except maybe her garters, and down below it says "Pensive" or "Evening in Paris." Skeeter sells them to artists, he says— he'll tell you that to your face—but he's always got a few left over for the boys at Bullen's.

Well, Skeeter goes on up front and starts in to study the slot machines. He don't never play them, just studies them. Somebody said he's writing a book about how to beat them, but I don't think he's got the mind for it, is my opinion.

Clyde is halfway into the next game when Skeeter comes back again. He has some of the boys with him now.

"All right, all right," Clyde says, stopping his game.

"You tell him, Skeeter," the boys says.

"Yeah, Skeeter, you tell me," Clyde says.

"Oh," Skeeter says, "it's just something some of them is saying, Clyde, is all."

"Who's saying?" Clyde says. "Who's saying what?"

"Some of them," Skeeter says, "over at the Arcade."

The Arcade, in case you don't know, is the other poolhall in town. Bullen's and the Arcade don't mix, and I guess Skeeter is about the only one that shows up regular in both places, on account of he's got customers in both places. I'd personally like to keep Skeeter out of Bullen's, but Clyde buys a lot of art studies off him and I can't say nothing.

After a spell of thinking Clyde says to Skeeter, "Spill it."

"May not be a word of truth to it, Clyde," Skeeter says. "You know how folks talk. And all I know is what I hear. Course I knowed a long time that Bailey nigger is a damn funny nigger. Nobody never did find out where he come from—St. Louis, Chicago, New York, for all anybody knowed. And if he's stone deef how can he hear to play the piano?"

"Damn the nigger," Clyde says. "What is they saying, them Arcade bastards!"

"Oh, not all of them is saying it, Clyde. Just some of them is saying it. Red Hynes, that tends bar at the El

Paso, and them. Saying maybe the nigger didn't get them scratches on his face for nothing. Saying maybe he was trying something funny. That's a damn funny nigger, Clyde, I don't care what you say. And when you get right down to it, Clyde, kind of stuck up like. Anyways some of them at the Arcade is saying maybe the nigger throwed Clara in the river and then fished her out just to cover up. Niggers is awful good at covering up, Clyde."

Clyde don't say nothing to this, but I can tell he is thinking plenty and getting mad at what he's thinking—plenty. It's real quiet at Bullen's now.

"Maybe," Clyde says, "maybe they is saying what he was covering up from?"

"Yeah, Clyde," Skeeter says. "Matter of fact, they is. Yeah, some of them is saying maybe the nigger *raped* her!"

Bang! Clyde cracks the table with his cue stick. It takes a piece of pearl inlay right out of the apron board of the good, new table. Nobody says nothing. Clyde just stares at all the chalk dust he raised.

Then Skeeter says, "Raped her first, rescued her later, is what they is saying."

"What you going to do, Clyde?" Banjo Wheeler says.

"Clyde is thinking!" I say. "Leave him think!" But personally I never seed Clyde take that long just to think.

"Move," Clyde says.

The boys give Clyde plenty of room. He goes over to the rack and tips a little talcum in his hands. The boys is all watching him good. Then Clyde spits. I am right by the cuspidor and can see Clyde's spit floating on the water inside. Nobody says nothing. Clyde's spit is going around in the water and I am listening to hear what he is going to do. He takes the chalk out of my hand. He still don't say nothing. It is the first time he ever chalks his cue with me around to do it.

Then he says, "What kind of nigger is this Bailey nigger, Roy?"

Roy—that's me.

"Oh, just a no-good nigger, Clyde," I say. "Plays the piano at the Louisiana Social Parlor—*some* social parlor,

Clyde—is about all I know, or anybody. Fishes quite a bit—just a lazy, funny, no-good nigger . . ."

"But he ain't no *bad* nigger, Roy?"

"Naw, he ain't *that*, Clyde," I say. "We ain't got none of them kind left in town."

"Well," Clyde says, "just so's he ain't no *bad* nigger."

Then, not saying no more, Clyde shoots and makes the ten ball in the side pocket. I don't have to tell you the boys is all pretty disappointed in Clyde. I have to admit I never knowed no other white man but Clyde to act like that. But maybe Clyde has his reasons, I say to myself, and wait.

Well, sir, that was right before the news come from the hospital. Ace is friendly with a nurse there is how we come to get it. He calls her on the phone to find out how Clara is. She is unconscious and ain't able to talk yet, but that ain't what makes all hell break loose at Bullen's. It's—un-mis-tak-able ev-i-dence of preg-nan-cy!

Get it? Means she was knocked up. Whoa! I don't have to tell you how that hits the boys at Bullen's. Some said they admired Clyde for not flying off the handle in the first place and some said they didn't, but all of them said they had let their good natures run away with their better judgments. They was right.

I goes to Ace, that's holding the kitty we took up for the nigger, and gets my quarter back. I have a little trouble at first as some of the boys has got there in front of me and collected more than they put in—or else Ace is holding out.

All this time Clyde is in the washroom. I try to hurry him up, but he don't hurry none. Soon as he unlocks the door and comes out we all give him the news.

I got to say this is the first time I ever seed Clyde act the way he do now. I hate to say it, but—I will. Clyde, he don't act much like a man. No, he don't, not a bit. He just reaches his cue down and hands it to me.

"Chalk it," he says. "Chalk it," is all he says. Damn if I don't almost hand it back to him.

I chalk his cue. But the boys, they can't stand no more. Ace says he is going to call the hospital again.

"Damn it, Clyde," Banjo says. "We got to do something.

Else they ain't going to be no white woman safe in the streets. What they going to think of you at the Arcade? I can hear Red Hynes and them laughing."

That is the way the boys is all feeling at Bullen's, and they say so. I am waiting with the rest for Clyde to hurry up and do something, or else explain hisself. But he just goes on, like nothing is the matter, and starts up a new game. It's awful quiet. Clyde gets the nine ball on the break. It hung on the lip of the pocket like it didn't want to, but it did.

"You sure like that old nine ball, Clyde," I say, trying to make Clyde feel easy and maybe come to his senses. I rack the nine for him. My hand is wet and hot and the yellow nine feels like butter to me.

"Must be the color of the nine is what he like," Banjo says.

Whew! I thought that would be all for Banjo, but no sir, Clyde goes right on with the game, like it's a compliment.

A couple of guys is whistling soft at what Banjo got away with. Me, I guess Clyde feels sorry for Banjo, on account of they is both fighters. Clyde was a contender for the state heavy title three years back, fighting under the name of Big Boy Bullen, weighing in at two thirty-three. Poor old Banjo is a broken-down carnival bum, and when he's drinking too heavy, like last night and every night, he forgets how old and beat up he is and don't know no better than to run against Clyde, that's a former contender and was rated in *Collyer's Eye*. Banjo never was no better than a welter when he was fighting and don't tip more than a hundred fifty-five right now. What with the drink and quail he don't amount to much no more.

And then Ace comes back from calling up the hospital and says, "No change; Clara's still unconscious."

"Combination," Clyde says. "Twelve ball in the corner pocket."

That's all Clyde has got to say. We all want to do something, but Banjo wants to do it the worst and he says, "No change, still unconscious. Knocked out and knocked up—by a nigger! Combination—twelve ball in the corner pocket!"

"Dummy up!" Clyde says. He slugs the table again and

ruins a cube of chalk. He don't even look at Banjo or none of us. I take the whisk broom and brush the chalk away the best I could, without asking Clyde to move.

"Thanks," Clyde says, still not seeing nobody.

I feel kind of funny on account of Clyde never says thanks for nothing before. I wonder is it the old Clyde or is he feeling sick. Then, so help me, Clyde runs the table, thirteen balls. Ace don't even get a shot that game.

But, like you guessed, the boys won't hold still for it no more and is all waiting for Clyde to do something. And Clyde don't have to be no mind reader to know it. He gets a peculiar look in his eye that I seed once or twice before and goes over to Banjo—to—guess what?—to shake his hand. Yes sir, Clyde has got his hand out and is smiling—smiling at Banjo that said what he said.

Banjo just stands there with a dumb look on his face, not knowing what Clyde is all about, and they shake.

"So I'm yella, huh, Banjo?" That's what Clyde says to Banjo.

I don't know if Banjo means to do it, or can't help it, but he burps right in Clyde's face.

Boom! Clyde hits Banjo twice in the chin and mouth quick and drops him like a handkerchief. Banjo is all over the floor and his mouth is hanging open like a spring is busted and blood is leaking out the one side and he has got some bridgework loose.

"Hand me the nine, Roy," Clyde says to me. I get the nine ball and give it to Clyde. He shoves it way into Banjo's mouth that is hanging open and bleeding good.

Then Clyde lets him have one more across the jaw and you can hear the nine ball rattle inside Banjo's mouth.

Clyde says, "Now some of you boys been itching for action all night. Well, I'm here to tell you I'm just the boy to hand it out. Tonight I just feel like stringing me up a black nigger by the light of the silvery moon! Let's get gaiting!"

Now that was the old Clyde for you. A couple of guys reaches fast for cue sticks, but I am in charge of them and the tables, and I say, "Lay off them cue sticks! Get some two by fours outside!"

So we leaves old Banjo sucking on the nine ball and piles

into all the cars we can get and heads down for the Louisiana Social Parlor. I am sitting next to Clyde in his car.

On the way Ace tells us when he called the hospital the second time he got connected with some doctor fella. Ace said this doctor was sore on account of Ace's girl, that's the nurse, give out information about Clara that she wasn't supposed to. But the doctor said as long as we all knowed so much about the case already he thought we ought to know it was of some months' standing, Clara's condition. Ace said he could tell from the way the doctor was saying it over and over that he was worried about what we was planning to do to the coon. Ace's girl must of copped out to him. But Ace said he thanked the doc kindly for his trouble and hung up and wouldn't give his right name when the doc wanted to know. We all knowed about the doctor all right—only one of them young intern fellas from Memphis or some place—and as for the some months' standing part we all knowed in our own minds what nigger bucks is like and him maybe burning with strong drink on top of it. Ace said he hoped the nurse wouldn't go and lose her job on account of the favor she done for us.

The only thing we seed when we gets to the Louisiana is one old coon by the name of Old Ivy. He is locking up. We asks him about Sleep Bailey, but Old Ivy is playing dumb and all he says is, "Suh? Suh?" like he don't know what we mean.

"Turn on them there lights," we says, "so's we can see." Old Ivy turns them on.

"Where's the crowd," we says, "that's always around?"

"Done went," Old Ivy says.

"So they's done went," Skeeter says. "Well, if they's trying to steal that piano-playing nigger away they won't get very far."

"No, they won't get very far with that," Clyde says. "Hey, just seeing all them bottles is got me feeling kind of dry-like."

So we gets Old Ivy to put all the liquor on the bar and us boys refreshes ourselfs. Skeeter tells Old Ivy to put some beer out for chasers.

Old Ivy says they is fresh out of cold beer.

"It don't have to be cold," Skeeter says. "We ain't proud."

Old Ivy drags all the bottled beer out on the bar with the other. Then he goes back into the kitchen behind the bar and we don't see him no more for a little.

"Hey, old nigger," Skeeter says. "Don't try and sneak out the back way."

"No, suh," Old Ivy says.

"Hey, Old Ivy," Clyde says. "You got something to eat back there?"

"Suh?" He just gives us that old *suh*. "Suh?"

"You heard him," Skeeter says.

"No, suh," Old Ivy says, and we seed him in the service window.

"Guess maybe he's deef," Skeeter says. "You old coon, I hope you ain't blind!" And Skeeter grabs a bottle of beer and lams it at Old Ivy's head. Old Ivy ducks and the big end of the bottle sticks in the wall and don't break. It is just beaverboard, the wall.

All us boys gets the same idee and we starts heaving the beer bottles through the window where Old Ivy was standing, but ain't no more.

"Hit the nigger baby!"

"Nigger in the fence!"

We keeps this up until we done run out of bottles, all except Skeeter that's been saving one. "Hey, wait," he says. "It's all right now, Grampaw. Come on, old boy, you can come out now."

But Old Ivy don't show hisself. I am wondering if he got hit on a rebound.

"Damn it, boy," Skeeter says. "Bring us some food. Or you want us to come back in there?"

"Suh?" It's that old *suh* again. "Yes, suh," Old Ivy says in the kitchen, but we don't see him.

Then we do. And Skeeter, he lets go the last bottle with all he's got. It hits Old Ivy right in the head. That was a mean thing Skeeter done, I think, but then I see it's only the cook's hat Old Ivy's got in his hand that got hit. He was holding it up like his head is inside, but it ain't.

The boys all laughs when they seed what Old Ivy done to fool Skeeter.

"Like in war when you fool the enemy," Clyde says.

"That's a smart nigger," I say.

"So that's a smart nigger, huh?" Skeeter says. "I'll take and show you what I do to smart niggers that gets smart with me!"

"Cut it out," Clyde says. "Leave him alone. He ain't hurting nothing. You just leave that old coon be." That is Clyde for you, always sticking up for somebody, even a nigger.

Clyde and me goes into the next room looking for a place to heave, as Clyde has got to. It is awful dark, but pretty soon our eyes gets used to it, and we can see some tables and chairs and a juke box and some beer signs on the walls. It must be where they do their dancing. I am just standing there ready to hold Clyde's head, as he is easing hisself, when I begins to hear a piano like a radio is on low. I can just barely pick it out, a couple a notes at a time, sad music, blues music, nigger music.

It ain't no radio. It is a piano on the other side of the room. I am ready to go and look into it when Clyde says, "It ain't nothing." Ain't nothing! Sometimes I can't understand Clyde for the life of me. But I already got my own idee about the piano.

About then Skeeter and Ace comes in the room yelling for Clyde in the dark, saying the boys out front is moving on to the next place. We hear a hell of a racket out by the bar, like they broke the mirror, and then it's pretty still and we know they is almost all left.

Skeeter gives us one more yell and Ace says, "Hey, Clyde, you fall in?" They is about to leave when Skeeter, I guess it is, hears the piano just like we been hearing it. All this time Clyde has got his hand over my mouth like he don't want me to say we is there.

Skeeter calls Old Ivy and says he should turn on the lights, and when Old Ivy starts that *suh* business again Skeeter lays one on him that I can hear in the dark.

So Old Ivy turns on the lights, a lot of creepy greens, reds, and blues. Then Clyde and me both seed what I already guessed—it's the Bailey nigger playing the piano—and Skeeter and Ace seed it is him and we all seed each other.

And right then, damn if the nigger don't start in to sing a song. Like he didn't know what was what! Like he didn't know what we come for! That's what I call a foxy nigger.

Skeeter yells at him to stop singing and to come away from the piano. He stops singing, but he don't move. So we all goes over to the piano.

"What's your name, nigger?" Skeeter says.

"Bailey," Sleep says, reading Skeeter's lips.

Old Ivy comes over and he is saying a lot of stuff like, "That boy's just a borned fool. Just seem like he got to put his foot in it some kind of way."

Sleep hits a couple a notes light on the piano that sounds nice and pretty.

"You know what we come for?" Skeeter says.

Sleep hits them same two notes again, nice and pretty, and shakes his head.

"Sure you don't know, boy?" Clyde says.

Sleep is just about to play them notes again when Skeeter hits him across the paws with a fungo bat. Then Sleep says, "I spect you after me on account of that Miss Beck I fish out of the river."

"That's right," Skeeter says. "You spect right."

"You know what they is saying uptown, Sleep?" I say.

"I heard," Sleep says.

"They is saying," I say, "you raped Clara and throwed her in the river to cover up."

"That's just a lie," Sleep says.

"Who says it's a lie?" Clyde says.

"That's just a white-folks lie," Sleep says. "It's God's truth."

"How you going to prove it?" Clyde says.

"Yeah," I say. "How you going to prove it?"

"How you going to prove it to them, son?" Old Ivy says.

"Here, ain't I?" Sleep says.

"Yeah, you's here all right, nigger," Skeeter says, "but don't you wish you wasn't!"

"If I'm here I guess I got no call to be scared," Sleep

says. "Don't it prove nothing if I'm here, if I didn't run away? Don't that prove nothing?"

"Naw," Skeeter says. "It don't prove nothing. It's just a smart nigger trick."

"Wait till Miss Beck come to and talk," Sleep says. "I ain't scared."

"No," Old Ivy says, "you ain't scared. He sure ain't scared a bit, is he, Mr. Bullen? That's a good sign he ain't done nothing bad, ain't it, Mr. Bullen?"

"Well," Clyde says. "I don't know about that. . . ."

Skeeter says, "You sure you feel all right, Clyde?"

"What you mean you don't know, Clyde?" Ace says. "Clara is knocked up and this is the bastard done it!"

"Who the hell else, Clyde?" I say. I wonder is Clyde dreaming or what.

"He ain't a bad boy like that, Mr. Bullen," Old Ivy says, working on Clyde.

"I tell you what," Clyde says.

"Aw, stop it, Clyde," Skeeter and Ace both says. "We got enough!"

"Shut up!" Clyde says and he says it like he mean it.

"Listen to what Mr. Bullen got to say," Old Ivy says.

"This is the way I seed it," Clyde says. "This ain't no open-and-shut case of rape—leastways not yet it ain't. Now the law——"

Skeeter cuts in and says, "Well, Clyde, I'll see you the first of the week." He acts like he is going to leave.

"Come back here," Clyde says. "You ain't going to tell no mob nothing till I got this Bailey boy locked up safe in the county jail waiting judgment."

"O.K., Clyde," Skeeter says. "That's different. I thought you was going to let him get away."

"Hell, no!" Clyde says. "We got to see justice did, ain't we?"

"Sure do, Clyde," Skeeter says.

Ace says, "He'll be nice and safe in jail in case we got to take up anything with him."

I knowed what they mean and so do Old Ivy. He says, "Better let him go right now, Mr. Bullen. Let him run for it. This other way they just going to bust in the jailhouse and take him out and hang him to a tree."

"The way I seed it," Clyde says, "this case has got to be handled according to the law. I don't want this boy's blood on my hands. If he ain't to blame, I mean."

"That's just what he ain't, Mr. Bullen," Old Ivy says. "But it ain't going to do no good to put him in that old jailhouse."

"We'll see about that," Clyde says.

"Oh, sure. Hell, yes!" Skeeter says. "We don't want to go and take the law in our own hands. That ain't our way, huh, Ace?"

"Cut it out," Clyde says.

"Maybe Miss Beck feel all right in the morning, son, and it going to be all right for you," Old Ivy says to Sleep. The old coon is crying.

So we takes Sleep in Clyde's car to the county jail. We makes him get down on the floor so's we can put our feet on him and guard him better. He starts to act up once on the way, but Skeeter persuades him with the fungo bat in the right place, *conk*, and he is pretty quiet then.

Right after we get him behind bars it happens.

Like I say, Clyde is acting mighty peculiar all night, but now he blows his top for real. That's what he does all right—plumb blows it. It is all over in a second. He swings three times—one, two, three—and Skeeter and Ace is out cold as Christmas, and I am holding this fat eye. Beats me! And I don't mind telling you I laid down quick with Skeeter and Ace, like I was out, till Clyde went away. Now you figure it out.

But I ain't preferring no charges on Clyde. Not me, that's his best friend, even if he did give me this eye, and Skeeter ain't, that needs Bullen's for his business, or Ace.

What happens to who? To the jig that said he pulled Clara out of the river?

You know that big old slippery elm by the Crossing? That's the one. But that ain't how I got the eye.

The Old Bird, A Love Story

Unemployed and elderly Mr. Newman sensed there were others, some of them, just as anxious as he was to be put on. But he was the oldest person in the room. He approached the information girl, and for all his show of business, almost brusqueness, he radiated timidity. The man in front of him asked the girl a question, which was also Mr. Newman's.

"Are they doing any hiring today?"

The girl gave the man an application, a dead smile, and told him to take a seat after he had filled it out.

An answer, in any event, ready on her lips, she regarded Mr. Newman. Mr. Newman thought of reaching for an application and saying, "Yes, I'll take a seat," making a kind of joke out of the coincidence—the fellow before him looking for a job, too—only he could see from the others who had already taken seats it was no coincidence. They all had that superior look of people out of work.

"Got an application there for a retired millionaire?" Mr. Newman said, attempting jauntiness. That way it would be easier for her to refuse him. Perhaps it was part of her job to weed out applicants clearly too old to be of any use to the company. Mr. Newman had a real horror of butting in where he wasn't wanted.

The girl laughed, making Mr. Newman feel like a regular devil, and handed him an application. The smile she gave him was alive and it hinted that things were already on a personal basis between him and her and the company.

"You'll find a pen at the desk," she said.

Mr. Newman's bony old hand clawed at his coat pocket and unsnapped a large ancient fountain pen. "I carry my own! See?" In shy triumph he held up the fountain pen, which was orange. He unscrewed it, put it together, and fingered it as though he were actually writing.

But the girl was doing her dead smile at the next one.

Mr. Newman went over to the desk. The application questioned him: Single? Married? Children of your own? Parents living? Living with parents? Salary (expect)? Salary (would take)? Mr. Newman made ready with his fountain pen and in the ensuing minutes he did not lie about his age, his abilities, or past earnings. The salary he expected was modest. He was especially careful about making blots with his pen, which sometimes flowed too freely. He had noted before he started that the application was one of those which calls for the information to be printed. This he had done. Under "DO NOT WRITE BELOW THIS LINE" he had not written.

Mr. Newman read the application over and rose to take it to the information girl. She pointed to a bench. Hesitating for a moment, Mr. Newman seemed bent on giving it to her. He sat down. He got up. His face distraught, he walked unsteadily over to the girl.

Before she could possibly hear him, he started to stammer, "I wonder . . . . maybe it will make a difference," his voice both appealing for her mercy and saying it was out of the question—indeed he did not desire it—that she should take a personal interest in him. Then he got control, except for his eyes, which, without really knowing it, were searching the girl's face for the live smile, like the first time.

"I used green ink," he said limply.

"Let's see." The girl took the application, gave both sides a darting scrutiny, looking for mistakes.

"Will it make any difference? If it does and I could have another application, I could——" Mr. Newman had his orange fountain pen out again, as though to match the green on its tip with the ink on the application and thus fully account for what had come about.

"Oh no, I think that'll be all right," the girl said, finally getting the idea. "We're not that fussy." Mr. Newman, however, still appeared worried. "No, that's fine—and neat, too," the girl said. "Mr. *Newman*." She had spoken his name and there was her live smile. Mr. Newman blushed, then smiled a little himself. With perspiring fingers he put the fountain pen together and snapped it in his pocket.

The girl returned the application. Mr. Newman, lingering on, longed to confide in her, to tell her something of himself—why, for instance, he always used green ink; how famous and familiar a few years ago the initials "C. N." in green had been at the old place. Like his friend Jack P. Ferguson (died a few years back, it was in the papers) and the telegram. "Telegram" Ferguson, he was called, because he was always too busy to write. Green ink and telegrams, the heraldry of business. He wanted to tell her of the old days—the time he met Elbert Hubbard and Charley Schwab at a banquet.

Then on this side of the old days he saw a busy girl, busy being busy, who could never understand, and he forced himself to give up hope.

"I thank you," he said, going quickly back to his place on the bench to wait. He sat there rereading his application. Under "DO NOT WRITE BELOW THIS LINE" were some curious symbols. He guessed at their significance: CLN (Clean?); DSPN (Disposition?); PRSNLTY (Personality, no doubt about that one); PSE (Poise?); FCW (?); LYL (Loyal?); PSBLE LDR (Possible Leader); NTC (?). His fingers were damp with perspiration, and for fear he would present an untidy application, he laid it on his lap and held his hands open at his sides, letting them get cool and dry in case he had to shake hands with the interviewer.

When they were ready to see him, Mr. Newman hustled into a small glass office and stood before a young man. A sign with wooden letters indicated that he was Mr. Shanahan. Mr. Shanahan was reading a letter. Mr. Newman did not look directly at Mr. Shanahan: it was none of Mr. Newman's business—Mr. Shanahan's letter—and he did not want to seem curious or expectant of immediate attention. This was their busy season.

Mr. Shanahan, his eyes still reading the letter, noiselessly extended a hand toward Mr. Newman. A moment later he moved his head and it was then that Mr. Newman saw the hand. Mr. Newman paled. Caught napping! A bad beginning. He hastened to shake Mr. Shanahan's hand, recoiled in time. Mr. Shanahan had only been reaching for the application. Mr. Newman handed it to Mr. Shanahan and said, "Thank you," for some reason.

"Ah, yes. Have a seat." Mr. Shanahan rattled the application in one hand. "What kind of work did you want to do?" Evidently he expected no answer, for he went on to say, "I don't have to tell you, Mr. Newman, there's a labor shortage, especially in nondefense industries. That, and that alone, accounts for the few jobs we have to offer. We're an old-line house."

"Yes," Mr. Newman said.

"And there aren't any office jobs," Mr. Shanahan continued. "That's the kind of work you've always done?"

"Yes, it is," Mr. Newman said. Mr. Shanahan sucked a tooth sadly.

Mr. Newman was ready now for the part about the company letting him know later.

"How'd you like a temporary job in our shipping room?" Mr. Shanahan said, his eyes suddenly watchful.

For an instant Mr. Newman succeeded in making it plain that he, like any man of his business experience, was meant for better things. A moment later, in an interesting ceremony which took place in his heart, Mr. Newman surrendered his well-loved white collar. He knew that Mr. Shanahan, with that dark vision peculiar to personnel men, had witnessed the whole thing.

"Well . . ." he said.

Mr. Shanhan, the game bagged and bumping from his belt, got cordial now. "How are you, pretty handy with rope?"

He said it in such a flattering way that Mr. Newman trembled under the desire to be worthy. "Yes, I am," he said.

"But can you begin right away?" It was the final test.

"Yes, I can!" Mr. Newman said, echoing some of Mr. Shanahan's spirit. "You bet I can!"

"Well then, follow me!"

Mr. Shanahan guided Mr. Newman through a maze of departments. On an elevator, going down, he revealed what the job paid to start. Mr. Newman nodded vigorously that one could not expect too much to start. Mr. Shanahan told him that he didn't have to tell him that they were a firm known far and wide for fair dealing and that if (for any reason) Mr. Newman ever left them, it should be easy to get another position, and . . . out of the elevator and in the lower depths, Mr. Shanahan said he would like to make sure Mr. Newman understood the job was only temporary. After the Christmas holidays things were pretty slow in their line. Otherwise, they would be glad to avail themselves of his services the year round. However, the experience Mr. Newman would get here might very well prove invaluable to him in later life. Mr. Newman nodded less vigorously now.

They came to a long table, flat against a wall, extending around a rafterish room fitted out for packing: tough twine and hairy manila rope on giant spools, brown paper on rollers, sticking tape bearing the company's name, crest, and slogan: "A modern house over 100 years *young.*"

Several men were packing things. Mr. Shanahan introduced Mr. Newman to one of them.

"This is your boss, Mr. Hurley. This is Mr. Newman. Mr. Newman's pretty handy with rope. Ought to make an A-1 packer."

"Well . . ." Mr. Newman said, embarrassed before the regular packers.

He shook Mr. Hurley's hard hand.

"I sure hope so," Mr. Hurley said grimly. "This is our busy season."

When Mr. Shanahan had gone Mr. Hurley showed Mr. Newman where he could hang his coat. He told him what he would have to do and what he would be held responsible for. He cited the sad case of the shipment sent out last week to Fargo, North Dakota. The company had lost exactly double the amount of the whole sale, to say nothing of good will. Why? Faulty packing! He urged Mr. Newman to figure it out for himself. He told Mr. Newman that haste made waste, but that they were expected to get incoming orders out of the house on the same day. Not tomorrow. Not the next day. The same day. Finally Mr. Hurley again brought up the case of the shipment sent to Fargo, and seemed pleased with the reaction it got. For Mr. Newman frowned his forehead all out of shape and rolled his head back and forth like a sad old bell, as if to say, "Can such things be?"

"All right, Newman, let's see what you can do!" Mr. Hurley slapped him on the shoulder like a football coach sending in a substitute. Mr. Newman, gritting his false teeth, tackled his first assignment for the company: a half-dozen sets of poker chips, a box of rag dolls, 5,000 small American flags, and a boy's sled going to Waupaca, Wisconsin.

Mr. Newman perspired . . . lost his breath, caught it, tried to break a piece of twine with his bare hands, failed, cut his nose on a piece of wrapping paper, bled, barked his shin on an ice skate, tripped, said a few cuss words to himself . . . perspired.

"We go to lunch at twelve in this section," Mr. Hurley told him in a whisper a few minutes before that time. "If you want to wash up, go ahead now."

But Mr. Newman waited until the whistle blew before he knocked off. He had a shipment he wanted to get off. It was ten after twelve when he punched out.

There was no crowd at the time clock and he had a chance to look the thing over. He tried to summon up a little interest, but all he felt with any intensity was the lone fact that he'd never had to punch a clock before. It had always been enough before that he live by one.

On his lunch hour he did not know where to go. The company had a place where you could eat your lunch, but Mr. Newman had neglected to bring one. Quite reasonably he had not anticipated getting a job and starting on it the same day. After the usual morning of looking around, he had expected to go home and eat a bite with Mrs. Newman.

He walked past a lunch stand twice before he could make certain, without actually staring in the window at the menu painted on the wall, that hamburgers were ten cents and coffee five. He entered the place, then, and ordered with assurance that he would not be letting himself in for more than he could afford. He did not have any money to spare. Would it be better, he wondered, to have payday come soon and get paid for a few days' work, or could he hold out for a week or so and really have something when he did get paid? Leaving the lunch stand, he walked in the direction of the company, but roundabout so he would not get back too soon. Say about fifteen minutes to one. That would give him time to go to the washroom.

"Where did you eat your lunch?" Mr. Hurley asked him the first thing. "I didn't see you in the lunchroom."

"Oh, I ate out," Mr. Newman said, gratified that he'd been missed until he saw that he had offended Mr. Hurley by eating out. "I didn't bring my lunch today," he explained. "Didn't think I'd be working so soon."

"Oh." But Mr. Hurley was still hurt.

"I heard they let you eat your lunch in the building," Mr. Newman said, giving Mr. Hurley his chance.

Mr. Hurley broke down and told Mr. Newman precisely where the employees' lunchroom was, where it wasn't, how to get there from the shipping room, how not to. There were two ways to get there, he said, and he guessed, as for him, he never went the same way twice in a row.

"You know how it is," Mr. Hurley laughed, tying it in with life.

In the end Mr. Newman was laughing with Mr. Hurley, "Well, I guess so." Talking with Mr. Hurley gave Mr. Newman a feeling of rare warmth. It was man-to-man or nothing with Hurley. He hoped there would be other lunch hours like this one. He went back to work at four minutes to one.

During the afternoon Mr. Newman worked up a dislike for the fat fellow next to him, but when they teamed up on a big shipment of toys the fat fellow made some cynical remarks about the company and Mr. Newman relaxed. His kind were harmless as rivals. Mr. Newman thought the company would be better off with employees like himself. And then he was ashamed, for at bottom he admired the fat fellow for his independence. Mr. Newman regretted that he was too old to be independent.

Toward the end of the day he was coming from getting a drink of water when he overheard Mr. Hurley talking with Mr. Shanahan.

"Yeah," Mr. Hurley said, "when you said the old bird

was handy with rope I thought, boy, he's old enough to think about using some on himself. My God, Shanahan, if this keeps up we'll have to draft them from the old people's home."

Mr. Newman, feeling indecently aged, unable to face them, went for another drink of water. He had to keep moving. When he returned to the shipping room they were all working and Mr. Shanahan was not there.

Just before quitting time, Mr. Hurley came over and congratulated him on his first day's work. He said he thought Mr. Newman would make out all right, and showed him an easier way to cut string. When he suggested that Mr. Newman wash up before the whistle blew, Mr. Newman did not have the faith to refuse. He could not look Mr. Hurley in the eye now and say something about wanting to finish up a shipment. Any extraordinary industry on his part, he knew now, was useless. He was too old. All they could see when they looked at him was an old man. That was the only fact about him. He was an old bird.

"All right, Charley, see you in the morning," Mr. Hurley said.

Mr. Newman slowly brought himself to realize he was "Charley" to Mr. Hurley. He had never before been "Charley" to anyone on such short acquaintance. Probably he would be "Old Charley" before long, which reminded him that Christmas was coming. There was no meaning beyond Christmas in all this sweat and humiliation, but that was enough. He would stick it out.

Mr. Newman was impressed again with the vaultlike solemnity of the washroom. The strange dignity of the toilet booths, the resounding marble chips in the floor, the same as statehouses, the plenitude of paper, the rude music of water coursing, the fat washbowls, all resplendent and perfect of their kind, and towels, white as winding sheets, circulating without end . . .

Mr. Newman, young here, luxuriated. Still he was sensible about it. The company was a big company and could no doubt stand a lot of wasting of towels and toilet paper, but Mr. Newman, wanting to be fair, took only what he needed of everything. He would not knowingly abuse a privilege. He read a notice concerning a hospitalization service the company offered the employees. The sensibleness of such a plan appealed strongly to Mr. Newman. He thought he would have to look into that, completely forgetting that he was only on temporary.

At the sound of the five-o'clock whistle Mr. Newman hurried out and took his place in the line of employees at the time clock. When his turn came to punch out, clutching his time card, he was shaking all over. The clock would jam, or stamp the time in the wrong place, or at the last moment, losing confidence in the way he was holding the card, after all his planning, he would somehow stick it in the wrong way. Then there would be shouts from the end of the line, and everybody would know it was all on account of an old bird trying to punch out.

Mr. Newman's heart stopped beating, his body followed a preconceived plan from memory in the lapse, and then his heart started up again. Mr. Newman, a new friend to the machine, had punched out smoothly. One of the mass of company employees heading for home, Mr. Newman, his old body at once tired and tingling, walked so briskly he passed any number of younger people in the corridors. His mood was unfamiliar to him, one of achievement and crazy gaiety. He recognized the information girl ahead of him, passed her, and said over his shoulder:

"Well, good night!"

She smiled in immediate reflex, but it was sobering to Mr. Newman, though she did say good night, that she did not seem to remember him very well, for it had not been the live smile.

At the outside door it was snowing. Mr. Newman bought a newspaper and let the man keep the two cents change. He meant to revive an old tradition with him by reading the paper on the streetcar. There was enough snow on the sidewalk to ease his swollen feet.

It was too crowded on the streetcar to open his paper and he had to stand all the way. His eyes on a placard, he considered the case of a man from Minneapolis who had got welcome relief. Hanging there on a strap, rocking with the elemental heave of the streetcar, he felt utterly weary, a gray old thing. What mattered above all else, though—getting a job—he had accomplished. This he told himself over and over until it became as real as his fatigue and mingled itself with the tortured noise of the streetcar.

His wife met him at the door. One glimpse of his face, he thought, was all she needed and she would know how to treat him tonight. Already she knew something was up and had seen the scratch on his nose. She only said:

"You stayed downtown all day, Charley."

"Yes, I did," he said.

She went to hang up his coat, hat, and scarf. He stepped across the familiar rug to the radiator. He stood there warming his hands and listening to her moving things in the kitchen. He could not bring himself to go there, as he did on any other night before supper, to talk of nothing important or particular, to let the water run till it got cold, to fill their glasses. He had too much to tell her tonight. He had forgotten to remove his rubbers.

"Come on now, Charley."

He took a few steps, hesitated a second, and went straight into the kitchen. He was immediately, as he knew he would be, uneasy. He could think of nothing insignificant to say. His eyes were not meeting hers. The glasses were filled with water. Suddenly he had to look at her. She smiled. It was hard to bear. He *did* have news. But now, he felt, she expected too much.

He bit his lips in irritation and snapped, "Why didn't you let me get the water?" That was beside the point, of course, but it gave him leeway to sit down at the table. He made a project of it. Trying to extend the note of normalcy, he passed things to her. He involved her subtly in passing them back. He wanted her to know there was a time and place for everything and now it was for passing. He invented an unprecedented interest in their silverware. His knife, fork, and spoon absorbed him.

"Where did we get this spoon?" he asked crossly.

It was all wasted. She had revamped her strategy. She appeared amused, and there was about her a determination deeper than his to wait forever. Her being so amused was what struck him as insupportable. He had a dismaying con-

viction that this was the truest condition of their married
life. It ran, more or less, but always present, right through
everything they did. She was the audience—that was something like it—and he was always on stage, the actor who was
never taken quite seriously by his audience, no matter how
heroic the role. The bad actor and his faithful but not
foolish audience. Always! As now! It was not a hopeless
situation, but only because she loved him.

She *did* love him. Overcome by the idea, he abandoned
his silence. He heard himself telling her everything. Not
exactly as it was, naturally, but still everything. Not at first
about his being handy with rope, nothing about being
"Charley" and an old bird, but quite frankly that he was
working in the shipping room instead of the office. About
Mr. Shanahan, the interviewer—how nice he was, in a way.
About the information girl who seemed to take quite an
interest in him and who, to his surprise, had said good night
to him. Mr. Hurley, his department head, and how to get
to the employees' lunchroom. The washroom, plenty of
soap and towels, a clean place—clean as her kitchen; she
should see it. Where he had lunch, not much of a place.
The fat fellow next to him at the table, not exactly loyal
to the company, but a very likable chap . . . and here—he
dug into his shirt pocket—was a piece of their sticking tape,
as she could see, with their name and trademark.

"'A modern house,'" she read, "'over 100 years young'
—*young*—well, that's pretty clever."

"Oh, they're an old-line firm," Mr. Newman said.

"I'll have to pack you a lunch then, Charley," she said.
She had finally got into the adventure with him.

"I bought a paper tonight," he said. "It's in the other
room."

With a little excited movement she parted the organdy
curtain at the window. "My, Charley, just look at that!"
Snowflakes tumbled in feathery confusion past the yellow
light burning in the court, wonderfully white against the
night, smothering the whole dirty, roaring, guilty city in
innocence and silence and beauty.

Mr. Newman squirmed warm inside the thought of everything he could think of—the snow falling, the glow in

the kitchen, landing the job, Christmas coming, her . . .

Their supper got cold.

She let the curtain fall together, breathing, "My!"

Reluctantly Mr. Newman assumed the duty he had as husband and only provider—not to be swept away by dreams and snowflakes. He said with the stern wisdom of his generation:

"Keeps up much longer it'll tie up transportation."

"But do you like that kind of work, Charley?"

He assured her most earnestly that he did, knowing she knew he'd do anything to get into an office again. He caught himself on the verge of telling her that working in the shipping room was just the way the company, since it was so old and reliable, groomed its new employees for service in the office. But that sounded too steep and ultimately disastrous. He had to confess it was only temporary work. This pained her, he could see, and he tried to get her mind on something else.

"I'll bet you had no idea your husband was so handy with rope."

He told her how it came on big spools, like telegraph wire. But she did not think this important.

"The people," he said, "the ones I've met at least— well, they all seem very nice."

"Then maybe they'll keep you after Christmas, Charley!"

He looked sharply at her and could tell she was sorry she said that. She understood what must follow. He opened his mouth to speak, said nothing, and then, closing his eyes to the truth, he said:

"Yes. You know, I think they will. I'm sure of it."

He coughed. That was not the way it was at all. It had happened again. He was the bad actor again. His only audience smiled and loved him.

Prince of Darkness

"I should've known you'd be eating breakfast, Father. But I was at your Mass and I said to myself that must be Father Burner. Then I stayed a few minutes after Mass to make my thanksgiving."

"Fine," Father Burner said. "Breakfast?"

"Had it, Father, thanking you all the same. It's the regret of my life that I can't be a daily communicant. Doctor forbids it. 'Fast every day and see how long you last,' he tells me. But I do make it to Mass."

"Fine. You say you live in Father Desmond's parish?"

"Yes, Father. And sometimes I think Father Desmond does too much. All the societies to look after. Plus the Scouts and the Legion. Of course Father Kells being so elderly and all . . ."

"We're all busy these days."

"It's the poor parish priest's day that's never done, I always say, Father, not meaning to slight the ladies, God love 'em."

Father Burner's sausage fingers, spelling his impatience over and over, worked up sweat in the folds of the napkin which he kept in view to provoke an early departure. "About this matter you say Father Desmond thought I might be interested in——"

"The Plan, Father." Mr. Tracy lifted his seersucker trousers by the creases, crossed his shining two-tone shoes, and rolled warmly forward. "Father . . ."

Father Burner met his look briefly. He was wary of the fatherers. A backslider he could handle, it was the old story, but a red-hot believer, especially a talkative one, could be a devilish nuisance. This kind might be driven away only by prayer and fasting, and he was not adept at either.

"I guess security's one thing we're all after."

Father Burner grunted. Mr. Tracy was too familiar to suit him. He liked his parishioners to be retiring, dumb, or frightened. There were too many references made to the priest's hard lot. Not so many poor souls as all that passed away in the wee hours, nor was there so much bad weather to brave. Mr. Tracy's heart bled for priests. That in itself was a suspicious thing in a layman. It all led up to the Plan.

"Here's the Plan, Father . . ." Father Burner watched his eye peel down to naked intimacy. Then, half listening, he gazed about the room. He hated it, too. A fabulous brown rummage of encyclopedias, world globes, maps, photographs, holy pictures, mirrors, crucifixes, tropical fish, and too much furniture. The room reproduced the world, all wonders and horrors, less land than water. From the faded precipices of the walls photographs viewed each other for the most part genially across time. Three popes, successively thinner, raised hands to bless their departed painters. The world globes simpered in the shadows, heavy-headed idiot boys, listening. A bird in a blacked-out cage scratched among its offal. An anomalous buddha peeked beyond his dusty umbilicus at the trampled figures in the rug. The fish swam on, the mirrors and encyclopedias turned in upon themselves, the earless boys heard everything and understood nothing. Father Burner put his big black shoe on a moth and sent dust flecks crowding up a shaft of sunlight to the distant ceiling.

"Say you pay in $22.67 every month, can be paid semi-annually or as you please, policy matures in twenty years and pays you $35.50 a month for twenty years or as long as you live. That's the deal for you, Father. It beats the deal Father Desmond's got, although he's got a darned good one, and I hope he keeps it up. But we've gone ahead in the last few years, Father. Utilities are sounder, bonds are more secure, and this new legislation protects you one hundred per cent."

"You say Ed—Father Desmond—has the Plan?"

"Oh, indeed, Father." Mr. Tracy had to laugh. "I hope

you don't think I'm trying to high-pressure you, Father.
It's not just a piece of business with me, the Plan."

"No?"

"No. You see, it's more or less a pet project of mine.
Hardly make a cent on it. Looking out after the fathers, you
might say, so they'll maybe look out after me—spiritually.
I call it heavenly life insurance."

Slightly repelled, Father Burner nodded.

"Not a few priests that I've sold the Plan to remember
me at the altar daily. I guess prayer's one thing we can all
use. Anyway, it's why I take a hand in putting boys through
seminary."

With that Mr. Tracy shed his shabby anonymity for
Father Burner, and grew executive markings. He became
the one and only Thomas Nash Tracy—T. N. T. It was impossible to read the papers and not know a few things about
T. N. T. He was in small loans and insurance. His company's advertising smothered the town and country; everybody knew the slogan "T. N. T. Spells Security." He
figured in any financial drive undertaken by the diocese,
was caught by photographers in orphanages, and sat at the
heavy end of the table at communion breakfasts. Hundreds
of nuns, thanks to his thoughtfulness, ate capon on Christmas Day, and a few priests of the right sort received
baskets of scotch. He was a B. C. L., a Big Catholic
Layman, and now Father Burner could see why. Father
Burner's countenance softened at this intelligence, and
T. N. T. proceeded with more assurance.

"And don't call it charity, Father. Insurance, as I said,
is a better name for it. I have a little money, Father, which
makes it possible." He tuned his voice down to a whisper. "You might say I'm moderately wealthy." He looked
sharply at Father Burner, not sure of his man. "But I'm
told there isn't any crime in that."

"I believe you need not fear for your soul on that
account."

"Glad to hear it from you, a priest, Father. Ofttimes
it's thrown up to me." He came to terms with reality,
smiling. "I wasn't always so well off myself, so I can understand the temptation to knock the other fellow."

"Fine."

"But that's still not to say that water's not wet or that names don't hurt sometimes, whatever the bard said to the contrary."

"What bard?"

" 'Sticks and stones——' "

"Oh."

"If this were a matter of faith and morals, Father, I'd be the one to sit back and let you do the talking. But it's a case of common sense, Father, and I think I can safely say, if you listen to me you'll not lose by it in the long run."

"It could be."

"May I ask you a personal question, Father?"

Father Burner searched T. N. T.'s face. "Go ahead, Mr. Tracy."

"Do you bank, Father?"

"*Bank?* Oh, bank—no. Why?"

"Let's admit it, Father," T. N. T. coaxed, frankly amused. "Priests as a class are an improvident lot—our records show it—and you're no exception. But that, I think, explains the glory of the Church down through the ages."

"The Church is divine," Father Burner corrected. "And the concept of poverty isn't exactly foreign to Christianity or even to the priesthood."

"Exactly," T. N. T. agreed, pinked. "But think of the future, Father."

Nowadays when Father Burner thought of the future it required a firm act of imagination. As a seminarian twenty years ago, it had all been plain: ordination, roughly ten years as a curate somewhere (he was not the kind to be sent to Rome for further study), a church of his own to follow, the fruitful years, then retirement, pastor emeritus, with assistants doing the spade work, leaving the fine touches to him, still a hearty old man very much alive. It was not an uncommon hope and, in fact, all around him it had materialized for his friends. But for him it was only a bad memory growing worse. He was the desperate assistant now, the angry functionary aging in the outer office. One day he would wake and find himself old, as the morning finds itself covered with snow. The future had assumed the

forgotten character of a dream, so that he could not be sure
that he had ever truly had one.

T. N. T. talked on and Father Burner felt a mist gener-
ating on his forehead. He tore his damp hands apart and
put the napkin aside. Yes, yes, it was true a priest received
miserably little, but then that was the whole idea. He did
not comment, dreading T. N. T.'s foaming compassion, to
be spat upon with charity. Yes, as a matter of fact, it would
be easier to face old age with something more to draw upon
than what the ecclesiastical authorities deemed sufficient
and would provide. Also, as T. N. T. pointed out, one never
knew when he might come down with an expensive illness.
T. N. T., despite himself, had something. . . . The Plan,
in itself, was not bad. He must not reject the olive branch
because it came by buzzard. But still Father Burner was a
little bothered by the idea of a priest feathering his nest.
Why? In other problems he was never the one to take the
ascetic interpretation.

"You must be between thirty-five and forty, Father."

"I'll never see forty again."

"I'd never believe it from anyone else. You sure don't
look it, Father."

"Maybe not. But I feel it."

"Worries, Father. And one big one is the future, Father.
You'll get to be fifty, sixty, seventy—and what have you got?
—not a penny saved. You look around and say to yourself—
where did it go?"

T. N. T. had the trained voice of the good and faithful
servant, supple from many such dealings. And still from
time to time a faint draught of contempt seemed to pass
through it which had something to do with his eyes. Here,
Father Burner thought, was the latest thing in simony, unnecessary, inspired from without, participated in spirit-
lessly by the priest who must yet suffer the brunt of the
blame and ultimately do the penance. Father Burner felt
mysteriously purchasable. He was involved in an exchange
of confidences which impoverished him mortally. In
T. N. T. he sensed free will in its senility or the infinite
capacity for equating evil with good—or with nothing—the
same thing, only easier. Here was one more word in the his-

tory of the worm's progress, another wave on the dry flood that kept rising, the constant aggrandizement of decay. In the end it must touch the world and everything at the heart. Father Burner felt weak from a nameless loss.

"I think I can do us both a service, Father."

"I don't say you can't." Father Burner rose quickly. "I'll have to think about it, Mr. Tracy."

"To be sure, Father." He produced a glossy circular. "Just let me leave this literature with you."

Father Burner, leading him to the door, prevented further talk by reading the circular. It was printed in a churchy type, all purple and gold, a dummy leaf from a medieval hymnal, and entitled, "A Silver Lining in the Sky." It was evidently meant for clergymen only, though not necessarily priests, as Father Burner could instantly see from its general tone.

"Very interesting," he said.

"My business phone is right on the back, Father. But if you'd rather call me at my home some night——"

"No thanks, Mr. Tracy."

"Allow me to repeat, Father, this isn't just business with me."

"I understand." He opened the door too soon for T. N. T. "Glad to have met you."

"Glad to have met you, Father."

Father Burner went back to the table. The coffee needed warming up and the butter had vanished into the toast. "Mary," he called. Then he heard them come gabbing into the rectory, Quinlan and his friend Keefe, also newly ordained.

They were hardly inside the dining room before he was explaining how he came to be eating breakfast so late—so late, see?—not *still*.

"You protest too much, Father," Quinlan said. "The Angelic Doctor himself weighed three hundred pounds, and I'll wager he didn't get it all from prayer and fasting."

"A pituitary condition," Keefe interjected, faltering. "Don't you think?"

"Yah, yah, Father, you'll wager"—Father Burner, eyes malignant, leaned on his knife, the blade bowing out bright and buttery beneath his fist—"and I'll wager you'll be the first saint to reach heaven with a flannel mouth!" Rising from the table, he shook Keefe's hand, which was damp from his pocket, and experienced a surge of strength, the fat man's contempt and envy for the thin man. He thought he might break Keefe's hand off at the wrist without drawing a drop of blood.

Quinlan stood aside, six inches or more below them, gazing up, as at two impossibly heroic figures in a hotel mural. Reading the caption under them, he mused, "Father Burner meets Father Keefe."

"I've heard about you, Father," Keefe said, plying him with a warmth beyond his means.

"Bound to be the case in a diocese as overstocked with magpies as this one." Father Burner threw a fresh napkin at a plate. "But be seated, Father Keefe." Keefe, yes, he had seen him before, a nobody in a crowd, some affair . . . the K. C. barbecue, the Youth Center? No, probably not, not Keefe, who was obviously not the type, too crabbed and introversive for Catholic Action. "I suppose," he said, "you've heard the latest definition of Catholic Action—the interference of the laity with the inactivity of the hierarchy."

"Very good," Keefe said uneasily.

Quinlan yanked off his collar and churned his neck up and down to get circulation. "Dean in the house? No? Good." He pitched the collar at one of the candles on the buffet for a ringer. "That turkey we met coming out the front door—think I've seen his face somewhere."

"Thomas Nash Tracy," Keefe said. "I thought you knew."

"The prominent lay priest and usurer?"

Keefe coughed. "They say he's done a lot of good."

Quinlan spoke to Father Burner: "Did you take out a policy, Father?"

"One of the sixth-graders threw a rock through his windshield," Father Burner said. "He was very nice about it."

"Muldoon or Ciesniewski?"

"A new kid. Public school transfer." Father Burner patted the napkin to his chin. "Not that I see anything wrong with insurance."

Quinlan laughed. "Let Walter tell you what happened to him a few days ago. Go ahead, Walter," he said to Keefe.

"Oh, that." Keefe fidgeted and, seemingly against his better judgment, began. "I had a little accident—was it Wednesday it rained so? I had the misfortune to skid into a fellow parked on Fairmount. Dented his fender." Keefe stopped and then, as though impelled by the memory of it, went on. "The fellow came raging out of his car at me. I thought there'd be serious trouble. Then he must have seen I was a priest, the way he calmed down, I mean. I had a funny feeling it wasn't because he was a Catholic or anything like that. As a matter of fact he wore a Masonic button." Keefe sighed. "I guess he saw I was a priest and ergo . . . knew I'd have insurance."

"Take nothing for your journey, neither staff, nor scrip," Quinlan said, "words taken from today's gospel."

Father Burner spoke in a level tone: "Not that I *still* see anything wrong with insurance. It's awfully easy," he continued, hating himself for talking drivel, "to make too much of little things." With Quinlan around he played the conservative; among the real right-handers he was the *enfant terrible*. He operated on the principle of discord at any cost. He did not know why. It was a habit. Perhaps it had something to do with being overweight.

Arranging the Dean's chair, which had arms, for himself, Quinlan sank into it, giving Keefe the Irish whisper. "Grace, Father."

Keefe addressed the usual words to God concerning the gifts they were about to receive. During the prayer Father Burner stopped chewing and did not reach for anything. He noted once more that Quinlan crossed himself sloppily enough to be a monsignor.

Keefe nervously cleared the entire length of his throat. "It's a beautiful church you have here at Saint Patrick's, Father." A lukewarm light appeared in his eyes, flickered, sputtered out, leaving them blank and blue. His endless fingers felt for his receding chin in the onslaught of silence.

"I have?" Father Burner turned his spoon abasingly to his bosom. "*Me?*" He jabbed at the grapefruit before him, his second, demolishing its perfect rose window. "I don't know why it is the Irish without exception are always laying personal claim to church property. The Dean is forever saying *my* church, *my* school, *my* furnace . . ."

"I'm sorry, Father," Keefe said, flushing. "And I'll confess I did think he virtually built Saint Patrick's."

"Out of the slime of the earth, I know. A common error." With sudden, unabated displeasure Father Burner recalled how the Dean, one of the last of the old brick and mortar pastors, had built the church, school, sisters' house, and rectory, and had named the whole thing through the lavish pretense of a popular contest. Opposed bitterly by Polish, German, and Italian minorities, he had effected a compromise between their bad taste (Saint Stanislaus, Saint Boniface, Saint Anthony) and his own better judgment in the choice of Saint Patrick's.

Quinlan, snorting, blurted, "Well, he did build it, didn't he?"

Father Burner smiled at them from the other world. "Only, if you please, in a manner of speaking."

"True," Keefe murmured humbly.

"Nuts," Quinlan said. "It's hard for me to see God in a few buildings paid for by the funds of the faithful and put up by a mick contractor. A burning bush, yes."

Father Burner, lips parched to speak an unsummonable cruelty, settled for a smoldering aside to the kitchen. "Mary, more eggs here."

A stuffed moose of a woman with a tabby-cat face charged in on swollen feet. She stood wavering in shoes sliced fiercely for corns. With the back of her hand she wiped some cream from the fuzz ringing her baby-pink mouth. Her hair poked through a broken net like stunted antlers. Father Burner pointed to the empty platter.

"Eggs," he said.

"Eggs!" she cried, tumbling her eyes like great blue dice among them. She seized up the platter and carried it whirling with grease into the kitchen.

Father Burner put aside the grapefruit. He smiled and spoke calmly. "I'll have to let the Dean know, Father, how much you like *his* plant."

"Do, Father. A beautiful church . . . 'a poem in stone'—was it Ruskin?"

"Ruskin? *Stones of Venice*," Father Burner grumbled. "*Sesame and Lilies*, I know . . . but I never cared for his *style*." He passed the knife lovingly over the pancakes on his plate and watched the butter bubble at the pores. "So much sweetness, so much light, I'm afraid, made Jack a dull boy."

Quinlan slapped all his pockets. "Pencil and paper, quick!"

"And yet . . ." Keefe cocked his long head, brow fretted, and complained to his upturned hands. "Don't understand how he stayed outside the Church." He glanced up hopefully. "I wonder if Chesterton gives us a clue."

Father Burner, deaf to such precious speculation, said, "In the nineteenth century Francis Thompson was the only limey worth his salt. It's true." He quartered the pancakes. "Of course, Newman."

"Hopkins has some good things."

"Good—yes, if you like jabberwocky and jebbies! I don't care for either." He dispatched a look of indictment at Quinlan.

"What a pity," Quinlan murmured, "Oliver Wendell couldn't be at table this morning."

"No, Father, you can have your Hopkins, you and Father Quinlan here. Include me out, as Sam Goldwyn says. Poetry—I'll take my poetry the way I take my liquor, neat."

Mary brought in the platter oozing with bacon and eggs.

"Good for you, Mary," Quinlan said. "I'll pray for you."

"Thank you, Father," Mary said.

Quinlan dipped the platter with a trace of obeisance to Father Burner.

"No thanks."

Quinlan scooped up the coffeepot in a fearsome rush and held it high at Father Burner, his arm so atremble the lid rattled dangerously. "Sure and will you be about having a sup of coffee now, Father?"

"Not now. And do you mind not playing the wild Irish wit so early in the day, Father?"

"That I don't. *But a relentless fate pursuing good Father*

Quinlan, he was thrown in among hardened clerics where but for the grace of God that saintly priest, so little understood, so much maligned . . ." Quinlan poured two cups and passed one to Keefe. "For yourself, Father."

Father Burner nudged the toast to Keefe. "Father Quinlan, that saintly priest, models his life after the Rover Boys, particularly Sam, the fun-loving one."

Quinlan dealt himself a mighty *mea culpa*.

Father Burner grimaced, the flesh rising in sweet, concentric tiers around his mouth, and said in a tone both entrusting and ennobling Keefe with his confidence, "The syrup, if you please, Father." Keefe passed the silver pitcher which was running at the mouth. Father Burner reimmersed the doughy remains on his plate until the butter began to float around the edges as in a moat. He felt them both watching the butter. Regretting that he had not foreseen this attraction, he cast about in his mind for something to divert them and found the morning sun coming in too strongly. He got up and pulled down the shade. He returned to his place and settled himself in such a way that a new chapter was indicated. "Don't believe I know where you're located, Father."

"Saint Jerome's," Keefe said. "Monsignor Fiedler's."

"One of those P. N. places, eh? Is the boss sorry he ever started it? I know some of them are."

Keefe's lips popped apart. "I don't quite understand."

Quinlan prompted: "P. N.—Perpetual Novena."

"Oh, I never heard him say."

"You wouldn't, of course. But I know a lot of them that are." Father Burner stuck a morsel on his fork and swirled it against the tide of syrup. "It's a real problem all right. I was all out for a P. N. here during the depression. Thought it might help. The Dean was against it."

"I can tell you this," Keefe said. "Attendance was down from what it used to be until the casualties began to come in. Now it's going up."

"I was just going to say the war ought to take the place of the depression." Father Burner fell silent. "Terrible thing, war. Hard to know what to do about it. I tried to sell the Dean the idea of a victory altar. You've seen them. Vigil lights——"

"At a dollar a throw," Quinlan said.

"Vigil lights in the form of a V, names of the men in the service and all that. But even that, I guess—— Well, like I said, I tried. . . ."

"Yes, it is hard," Keefe said.

"God, the Home, and the Flag," Quinlan said. "The poets don't make the wars."

Father Burner ignored that. "Lately, though, I can't say how I feel about P. N.'s. Admit I'm not so strong for them as I was once. Ought to be some way of terminating them, you know, but then they wouldn't be perpetual, would they?"

"No, they wouldn't," Keefe said.

"Not *so* perpetual," Quinlan said.

"Of course," Father Burner continued, "the term itself, perpetual novena, is preposterous, a solecism. Possibly dispensation lies in that direction. I'm not theologian enough to say. Fortunately it's not a problem we have to decide." He laid his knife and fork across the plate. "Many are the consolations of the lowly curate. No decisions, no money worries."

"We still have to count the sugar," Quinlan said. "And put up the card tables."

"Reminds me," Father Burner said earnestly. "Father Desmond at Assumption was telling me they've got a new machine does all that."

"Puts up card tables?" Quinlan inquired.

"Counts the collection, wraps the silver," Father Burner explained, "so it's all ready for the bank. Mean to mention it to the Dean, if I can catch him right."

"I'm afraid, Father, he knows about it already."

Father Burner regarded Quinlan skeptically. "Does? I suppose he's against it."

"I heard him tell the salesman that's what he had his assistants for."

"Assistant, Father, not assistants. You count the collection, not me. I was only thinking of you."

"I was only quoting him, Father. *Sic.* Sorry."

"Not at all. I haven't forgotten the days I had to do it. It's a job has to be done and nothing to be ashamed of. Wouldn't you say, Father Keefe?"

"I dare say that's true."

Quinlan, with Father Burner still molesting him with his eyes, poured out a glass of water and drank it all. "I still think we could do with a lot less calculating. I notice the only time we get rid of the parish paper is when the new lists are published—the official standings. Of course it's a lousy sheet anyway."

Father Burner, as editor of the paper, replied: "Yes, yes, Father. We all know how easy it is to be wrathful or fastidious about these things—or whatever the hell it is you are. And we all know there *are* abuses. But contributing to the support of the Church is still one of her commandments."

"Peace, Père," Quinlan said.

"Figures don't lie."

"Somebody was telling me just last night that figures do lie. He looked a lot like you."

Father Burner found his cigarettes and shuffled a couple half out of the pack. He eyed Quinlan and the cigarettes as though it were as simple to discipline the one as to smoke the others. "For some reason, Father, you're damned fond of those particular figures."

Keefe stirred. "Which particular figures, Fathers?"

"It's the figures put out by the Cardinal of Toledo on how many made their Easter duty last year." Father Burner offered Keefe a cigarette. "I discussed the whole thing with Father Quinlan last night. It's his latest thesis. Have a cigarette?"

"No, thanks," Keefe said.

"So you don't smoke?" Father Burner looked from Keefe to Quinlan, blacklisting them together. He held the cigarette hesitantly at his lips. "It's all right, isn't it?" He laughed and touched off the match with his thumbnail.

"His Eminence," Quinlan said, "reports only fifteen per cent of the women and five per cent of the men made their Easter duty last year."

"So that's only three times as many women as men,"

Father Burner said with buried gaiety. "Certainly to be expected in any Latin country."

"But fifteen per cent, Father! And five per cent! Just think of it!" Keefe glanced up at the ceiling and at the souvenir plates on the molding, as though to see inscribed along with scenes from the Columbian Exposition the day and hour the end of the world would begin. He finally stared deep into the goldfish tank in the window.

Father Burner plowed up the silence, talking with a mouthful of smoke. "All right, all right, I'll say what I said in the first place. There's something wrong with the figures. A country as overwhelmingly Catholic as Spain!" He sniffed, pursed his lips, and said, "Pooh!"

"Yes," Keefe said, still balking. "But it *is* disturbing, Father Burner."

"Sure it's disturbing, Father Keefe. *Lots* of things *are*."

A big, faded goldfish paused to stare through the glass at them and then with a single lob of its tail slipped into a dark green corner.

Quinlan said, "Father Burner belongs to the school that's always seeing a great renascence of faith in the offing. The hour before dawn and all that. Tell it to Rotary on Tuesday, Father."

Father Burner countered with a frosty pink smile. "What would I ever do without you, Father? If you're trying to say I'm a dreadful optimist, you're right and I don't mind at all. I am—and proud of it!"

Ascending to his feet, he went to the right side of the buffet, took down the card index to parishioners, and returned with it to his place. He pushed his dishes aside and began to sort out the deadheads to be called on personally by him or Quinlan. The Dean, like all pastors, he reflected, left the dirty work to the assistants. "Why doesn't he pull them," he snapped, tearing up a card, "when they kick off! Can't very well forward them to the next world. Say, how many Gradys live at 909 South Vine? Here's Anna, Catherine, Clement, Gerald, Harvey, James A., James F. —which James is the one they call 'Bum'?"

"James F.," Quinlan said. "Can't you tell from the take? The other James works."

"John, Margaret, Matthew—that's ten, no eleven. Here's Dennis out of place. Patrick, Rita and William—fourteen of them, no birth control there, and they all give. Except Bum. Nice account otherwise. Can't we find Bum a job? What's it with him, drink?"

Now he came to Maple Street. These cards were the remains of little Father Vicci's work among the magdalens. Ann Mason, Estelle Rogers, May Miller, Billie Starr. The names had the generic ring. Great givers when they gave— Christmas, $25; Easter, $20; Propagation of the Faith, $10; Catholic University, $10—but not much since Father Vicci was exiled to the sticks. He put Maple Street aside for a thorough sifting.

The doorbell rang. Father Burner leaned around in his chair. "Mary." The doorbell rang again. Father Burner bellowed. "Mary!"

Quinlan pushed his chair away from the table. "I'll get it."

Father Burner blocked him. "Oh, I'll get it! Hell of a bell! Why does he have a bell like that!" Father Burner opened the door to a middle-aged woman whose name he had forgotten or never known. "Good morning," he said. "Will you step in?"

She stayed where she was and said, "Father, it's about the servicemen's flag in church. My son Stanley—you know him——"

Father Burner, who did not know him, half nodded. "Yes, how is Stanley?" He gazed over her shoulder at the lawn, at the dandelions turning into poppies before his eyes.

"You know he was drafted last October, Father, and I been watching that flag you got in church ever since, and it's still the same, five hundred thirty-six stars. I thought you said you put a star up for all them that's gone in the service, Father."

Now the poppies were dandelions again. He could afford to be firm with her. "We can't spend all our time putting up stars. Sometimes we fall behind. Besides, a lot of the boys are being discharged."

"You mean there's just as many going in as coming out, so you don't have to change the flag?"

"Something like that."

"I see." He was sorry for her. They had run out of stars. He had tried to get the Dean to order some more, had even offered . . . and the Dean had said they could use up the gold ones first. When Father Burner had objected, telling him what it would mean, he had suggested that Father Burner apply for the curatorship of the armory.

"The pastor will be glad to explain how it works the next time you see him."

"Well, Father, if that's the way it is . . ." She was fading down the steps. "I just thought I'd ask."

"That's right. There's no harm in asking. How's Stanley?"

"Fine, and thank you, Father, for your trouble."

"No trouble."

When he came back to the table they were talking about the junior clergyman's examinations which they would take for the first time next week. Father Burner interrupted, "The Dean conducts the history end of it, you know."

"I say!" Keefe said. "Any idea what we can expect?"

"You have nothing to fear. Nothing."

"Really?"

"Really. Last year, I remember, there were five questions and the last four depended on the first. So it was really only one question—if you knew it. I imagine you would've." He paused, making Keefe ask for it.

"Perhaps you can recall the question, Father?"

"Perfectly, Father. 'What event in the American history of the Church took place in 1541?'" Father Burner, slumping in his chair, smirked at Keefe pondering for likely martyrs and church legislation. He imagined him skipping among the tomes and statuary of his mind, winnowing dates and little known facts like mad, only at last to emerge dusty and downcast. Father Burner sat up with a jerk and assaulted the table with the flat of his hand. "Time's up. Answer: 'De Soto sailed up the Mississippi.'"

Quinlan snorted. Keefe sat very still, incredulous, silent, utterly unable to digest the answer, finally croaking, "How

odd." Father Burner saw in him the boy whose marks in
school had always been a consolation to his parents.

"So you don't have to worry, Father. No sense in prepar-
ing for it. Take in a couple of movies instead. And cheer
up! The Dean's been examining the junior clergy for
twenty-five years and nobody ever passed history yet. You
wouldn't want to be the first one."

Father Burner said grace and made the sign of the cross
with slow distinction. "And, Father," he said, standing, extending his hand to Keefe, who also rose, "I'm glad to have
met you." He withdrew his hand before Keefe was through
with it and stood against the table knocking toast crumbs
onto his plate. "Ever play any golf? No? Well, come and
see us for conversation then. You don't have anything
against talking, do you?"

"Well, of course, Father, I . . ."

Father Burner gave Keefe's arm a rousing clutch. "Do
that!"

"I will, Father. It's been a pleasure."

"Speaking of pleasure," Father Burner said, tossing
Quinlan a stack of cards, "I've picked out a few lost sheep
for you to see on Maple Street, Father."

II. NOON

He hung his best black trousers on a hanger in the closet
and took down another pair, also black. He tossed them
out behind him and they fell patched at the cuffs and baggy
across his unmade bed. His old suède jacket, following, slid
dumpily to the floor. He stood gaping in his clerical vest
and undershorts, knees knocking and pimply, thinking
. . . what else? His aviator's helmet. He felt all the hooks
blindly in the darkness. It was not there. "Oh, hell!" he
groaned, sinking to his knees. He pawed among the old
shoes and boxes and wrapping paper and string that he
was always going to need. Under his golf bag he found it.
So Mary had cleaned yesterday.

There was also a golf ball unknown to him, a Royal
Bomber, with one small hickey in it. Father Desmond, he

remembered, had received a box of Royal Bombers from a thoughtful parishioner. He stuck the helmet on his balding head to get it out of the way and took the putter from the bag. He dropped the ball at the door of the closet. Taking his own eccentric stance—a perversion of what the pro recommended and a dozen books on the subject—he putted the ball across the room at a dirty collar lying against the bookcase. A thready place in the carpet caused the ball to jump the collar and to loose a pamphlet from the top of the bookcase. He restored the pamphlet—Pius XI on "Atheistic Communism"—and poked the ball back to the door of the closet. Then, allowing for the carpet, he drove the ball straight, *click*, through the collar, *clop*. Still had his old putting eye. And his irons had always been steady if not exactly crashing. It was his woods, the tee shots, that ruined his game. He'd give a lot to be able to hit his woods properly, not to dub his drives, if only on the first tee—where there was always a crowd (mixed).

At one time or another he had played every hole at the country club in par or less. Put all those pars and birdies together, adding in the only two eagles he'd ever had, and you had the winning round in the state open, write-ups and action shots in the papers—photo shows Rev. Ernest "Boomer" Burner, par-shattering padre, blasting out of a trap. He needed only practice perhaps and at his earliest opportunity he would entice some of the eighth-grade boys over into the park to shag balls. He sank one more for good measure, winning a buck from Ed Desmond who would have bet against it, and put the club away.

Crossing the room for his trousers he noticed himself in the mirror with the helmet on and got a mild surprise. He scratched a little hair down from underneath the helmet to offset the egg effect. He searched his eyes in the mirror for a sign of ill health. He walked away from the mirror, as though done with it, only to wheel sharply so as to see himself as others saw him, front and profile, not wanting to catch his eye, just to see himself. . . .

Out of the top drawer of the dresser he drew a clean white silk handkerchief and wiped the shine from his nose. He chased his eyes over into the corner of the mirror and saw nothing. Then, succumbing to his original intention, he knotted the handkerchief at the crown of the helmet and completed the transformation of time and place and person by humming, vibrato, "Jeannine, I dream in lilac time," remembering the old movie. He saw himself over his shoulder in the mirror, a sad war ace. It reminded him that his name was not Burner, but Boerner, an impediment removed at the outset of the first world war by his father. In a way he resented the old man for it. They had laughed at the seminary; the war, except as theory, hardly entered there. In perverse homage to the old Boerner, to which he now affixed a proud "von," he dropped the fair-minded American look he had and faced the mirror sneering, scar-cheeked, and black of heart, the flying Junker who might have been. "*Himmelkreuzdonnerwetter!* When you hear the word 'culture,'" he snarled, hearing it come back to him in German, "reach for your revolver!"

Reluctantly he pulled on his black trousers, falling across the bed to do so, as though felled, legs heaving up like howitzers.

He lay still for a moment, panting, and then let the innerspring mattress bounce him to his feet, a fighter coming off the ropes. He stood looking out the window, buckling his belt, and then down at the buckle, chins kneading softly with the effort, and was pleased to see that he was holding his own on the belt, still a good half inch away from last winter's high-water mark.

At the sound of high heels approaching on the front walk below, he turned firmly away from the window and considered for the first time since he posted it on the wall the prayer for priests sent him by a candle concern. "Remember, O most compassionate God, that they are but weak and frail human beings. Stir up in them the grace of their vocation which is in them by the imposition of the Bishops' hands. Keep them close to Thee, lest the enemy prevail against them, so that they may never do anything in the slightest degree unworthy of their sublime . . ." His eyes raced through the prayer and out the window. . . .

He was suddenly inspired to write another letter to the Archbishop. He sat down at his desk, slipped a piece of paper into his portable, dated it with the saint's day it was, and wrote, "Your Excellency: Thinking my letter of some months ago may have gone amiss, or perhaps due to the press of business——" He ripped the paper from the portable and typed the same thing on a fresh sheet until he came to "business," using instead "affairs of the Church." He went on to signify—it was considered all right to "signify," but to re-signify?—that he was still of the humble opinion that he needed a change of location and had decided, since he believed himself ready for a parish of his own, a rural one might be best, all things considered (by which he meant easier to get). He, unlike some priests of urban upbringing and experience, would have no objection to the country. He begged to be graced with an early reply. That line, for all its seeming docility, was full of dynamite and ought to break the episcopal silence into which the first letter had dissolved. This was a much stronger job. He thought it better for two reasons: the Archbishop was supposed to like outspoken people, or, that being only more propaganda talked up by the sycophants, then it ought to bring a reply which would reveal once and for all his prospects. Long overdue for the routine promotion, he had a just cause. He addressed the letter and placed it in his coat. He went to the bathroom. When he came back he put on the coat, picked up the suède jacket and helmet, looked around for something he might have forgot, a book of chances, a box of Sunday envelopes to be delivered, some copy for the printer, but there was nothing. He lit a cigarette at the door and not caring to throw the match on the floor or look for the ashtray, which was out of sight again, he dropped it in the empty holy-water font.

Downstairs he paused at the telephone in the hall, scribbled "Airport" on the message pad, thought of crossing it out or tearing off the page, but since it was dated he let it stand and added "Visiting the sick," signing his initials, E. B.

He went through the wicker basket for mail. A card from the Book-of-the-Month Club. So it was going to be another war book selection this month. Well, they knew what they could do with it. He wished the Club would wake up and select some dandies, as they had in the past. He thought of *Studs Lonigan*—there was a book, the best thing since the Bible.

An oblique curve in the road: perfect, wheels parallel with the center line. So many drivers took a curve like that way over on the other fellow's side. Father Burner touched the lighter on the dashboard to his cigarette and plunged his hams deeper into the cushions. A cloud of smoke whirled about the little Saint Christopher garroted from the ceiling. Father Burner tugged viciously at both knees, loosening the binding black cloth, easing the seat. Now that he was in open country he wanted to enjoy the scenery— God's majesty. How about a sermon that would liken the things in the landscape to the people in a church? All different, all the same, the handiwork of God. Moral: it is right and meet for rocks to be rocks, trees to be trees, pigs to be pigs, but—and here the small gesture that says so much—what did that mean that men, created in the image and likeness of God, should be? And what—— He thrust the sermon out of mind, tired of it. He relaxed, as before an open fireplace, the weight of dogma off his shoulders. Then he grabbed at his knees again, cursing. Did the tailor skimp on the cloth because of the ecclesiastical discount?

A billboard inquired: "Pimples?" Yes, he had a few, but he blamed them on the climate, the humidity. Awfully hard for a priest to transfer out of a diocese. He remembered the plan he had never gone through with. Would it work after all? Would another doctor recommend a change? Why? He would only want to know why, like the last bastard. Just a slight case of obesity, Reverend. Knew he was a non-Catholic when he said Reverend. Couldn't trust a Catholic one. Some of them were thicker than thieves with the clergy. Wouldn't want to be known as a malingerer, along with everything else.

Another billboard: "Need Cash? See T. N. T."

Rain. He knew it. No flying for him today. One more day between him and a pilot's license. Thirteen hours yet and it might have been twelve. Raining so, and with no flying, the world seemed to him . . . a valley of tears. He would drive on past the airport for a hamburger. If he had known, he would have brought along one of the eighth-grade boys. They were always bragging among themselves about how many he had bought them, keeping score. One of them, the Cannon kid, had got too serious from the hamburgers. When he said he was "contemplating the priesthood" Father Burner, wanting to spare him the terrible thing a false vocation could be, had told him to take up aviation instead. He could not forget the boy's reply: *But couldn't I be a priest like you, Father?*

On the other hand, he was glad to be out driving alone. Never had got the bang out of playing with the kids a priest in this country was supposed to. The failure of the Tom Playfair tradition. He hated most sports. Ed Desmond was a sight at a ball game. Running up and down the base lines, giving the umpires hell, busting all the buttons off his cassock. Assumption rectory smelled like a locker room from all the equipment. Poor Ed.

The rain drummed on the engine hood. The windshield wiper sliced back and forth, reminding him a little of a guillotine. Yes, if he had to, he would die for the Faith.

From here to the hamburger place it was asphalt and slicker than concrete. Careful. Slick. Asphalt. Remembered . . . Quinlan coming into his room one afternoon last winter when it was snowing—the idiot—prating:

> *Here were decent godless people:*
> *Their only monument the asphalt road*
> *And a thousand lost golf balls . . .*

That was Quinlan for you, always spouting against the status quo without having anything better to offer. Told him that. Told him golfers, funny as it might seem to some people, have souls and who's to save them? John Bosco worked wonders in taverns, which was not to say Father Burner thought he was a saint, but rather only that he was not too proud to meet souls halfway wherever it might be, in the confessional or on the fairways. Saint Ernest Burner, Help of Golfers, Pray for Us! (Quinlan's comeback.) Quinlan gave him a pain. Keefe, now that he knew what he was like, ditto. Non-smokers. Jansenists. First fervor is false fervor. They would cool. He would not judge them, however.

He slowed down and executed a sweeping turn into the parking lot reserved for patrons of the hamburger. He honked his horn his way, three shorts and a long—victory. She would see his car or know his honk and bring out two hamburgers, medium well, onions, pickle, relish, tomato, catsup—his way.

She came out now, carrying an umbrella, holding it ostensibly more over the hamburgers than herself. He took the tray from her. She waited dumbly, her eyes at a level with his collar.

"What's to drink?"

"We got pop, milk, coffee . . ." Here she faltered, as he knew she would, washing her hands of what recurrent revelation, rather than experience, told her was to follow.

"A nice cold bottle of beer." Delivered of the fatal words, Father Burner bit into the smoking hamburger. The woman turned sorrowfully away. He put her down again for native Protestant stock.

When she returned, sheltering the bottle under the umbrella, Father Burner had to smile at her not letting pious scruples interfere with business, another fruit of the so-called Reformation. Watch that smile, he warned himself, or she'll take it for carnal. He received the bottle from her hands. For all his familiarity with the type, he was uneasy. Her lowered eyes informed him of his guilt.

Was he immoderate? Who on earth could say? *In dubiis libertas*, not? He recalled his first church supper at Saint Patrick's, a mother bringing her child to the Dean's table. She's going to be confirmed next month, Monsignor. Indeed? Then tell me, young lady, what are the seven capital sins? Pride, Covetousness . . . Lust, Anger. Uh. The child's mother, one of those tough Irish females built like a robin, worried to death, lips silently forming the other sins for her daughter. Go ahead, dear. Envy. Proceed, child. Yes, Monsignor. Uh . . . Sloth. To be sure. That's six. One more. And . . . uh. Fear of the Lord, perhaps? Meekness? Hey, Monsignor, ain't them the Divine Counsels! The Dean, smiling, looking at Father Burner's plate, covered with chicken bones, at his stomach, fighting the vest, and for a second into the child's eyes, slipping her the seventh sin. *Gluttony*, Monsignor! The Dean gave her a coin for her trouble and she stood awkwardly in front of Father Burner, lingering, twisting her gaze from his plate to his stomach, to his eyes, finally quacking, Oh Fawther!

Now he began to brood upon his failure as a priest. There was no sense in applying the consolations of an anchorite to himself. He wanted to know one thing: when would he get a parish? When would he make the great metamorphosis from assistant to pastor, from mouse to rat, as the saying went? He was forty-three, four times transferred, seventeen years an ordained priest, a curate yet and only. He was the only one of his class still without a parish. The only one . . . and in his pocket, three days unopened, was another letter from his mother, kept waiting all these years, who was to have been his housekeeper. He could not bear to warm up her expectations again.

Be a chaplain? That would take him away from it all and there was the possibility of meeting a remote and glorious death carrying the Holy Eucharist to a dying soldier. It would take something like that to make him come out even, but then that, too, he knew in a corner of his heart, would be only exterior justification for him, a last bid for public approbation, a short cut to nothing. And the chaplain's job, it was whispered, could be an ordeal both ignominious and tragic. It would be just his luck to draw an assignment in a rehabilitation center, racking pool balls and repairing ping-pong bats for the boys—the apostolic gameroom attendant and toastmaster. Sure, Sarge, I'll lay you even money the Sox make it three straight in Philly and spot you a run a game to boot. You win, I lose a carton of Chesters—I win, you go to Mass every day for a week! Hardheaded holiness. . . .

There was the painful matter of the appointment to Saint Patrick's. The Dean, an irremovable pastor, and the Archbishop had argued over funds and the cemetery association. And the Archbishop, losing though he won, took his revenge, it was rumored, by appointing Father Burner as the

Dean's assistant. It was their second encounter. In the first days of his succession, the Archbishop heard that the Dean always said a green Mass on Saint Patrick's Day, thus setting the rubrics at nought. Furious, he summoned the Dean into his presence, but stymied by the total strangeness of him and his great age, he had talked of something else. The Dean took a different view of his narrow escape, which is what the chancery office gossips called it, and now every year, on repeating the error, he would say to the uneasy nuns, "Sure and nobody ever crashed the gates of hell for the wearing of the green." (Otherwise it was not often he did something to delight the hearts of the professional Irish.)

In the Dean's presence Father Burner often had the sensation of confusion, a feeling that someone besides them stood listening in the room. To free himself he would say things he neither meant nor believed. The Dean would take the other side and then . . . there they were again. The Dean's position in these bouts was roughly that of the old saints famous for their faculty of smelling sins and Father Burner played the role of the one smelled. It was no contest. If the Archbishop could find no words for the Dean there was nothing he might do. He might continue to peck away at a few stray foibles behind the Dean's back. He might point out how familiar the Dean was with the Protestant clergy about town. He did. It suited his occasional orthodoxy (reserved mostly to confound his critics and others much worse, like Quinlan, whom he suspected of having him under observation for humorous purposes) to disapprove of all such questionable ties, as though the Dean were entertaining heresy, or at least felt kindly toward this new "interfaith" nonsense so dear to the reformed Jews and fresh-water sects. It was very small game, however. And the merest brush with the Dean might bring any one of a hundred embarrassing occasions back to life, and it was easy for him to burn all over again.

When he got his darkroom rigged up in the rectory the Dean had come snooping around and inquired without staying for an answer if the making of tintypes demanded that a man shun the light to the extent Father Burner appeared to. Now and again, hearkening back to this episode, the Dean referred to him as the Prince of Darkness. It did not end there. The title caught on all over the diocese. It was not the only one he had.

In reviewing a new historical work for a national Catholic magazine, he had attempted to get back at two Jesuits he knew in town, calling attention to certain tendencies—he meant nothing so gross as "order pride"—which, if not necessarily characteristic of any religious congregation within the Church, were still too often to be seen in any long view of history (which the book at hand did not pretend to take), and whereas the secular clergy, *per se*, had much to answer for, was it not true, though certainly not through any superior virtue, nor even as a consequence of their secularity—indeed, he would be a fool to dream that such orders as those founded, for instance, by Saint Benedict, Saint Francis, and Saint Dominic (Saint Ignatius was not instanced) were without their places in the heart of the Church, even today, when perhaps . . .

Anyway "secular" turned up once as "circular" in the review. The local Jesuits, writing in to the magazine as a group of innocent bystanders, made many subtle plays upon the unfortunate "circular" and its possible application to the person of the reviewer (their absolute unfamiliarity with the reviewer, they explained, enabled them to indulge in such conceivably dangerous whimsey). But the direction of his utterances, they thought, seemed clear, and they regretted more than they could say that the editors of an otherwise distinguished journal had found space for them, especially in wartime, or perhaps they did not rightly comprehend the course—was it something new?—set upon by the editors and if so . . .

So Father Burner was also known as "the circular priest" and he had not reviewed anything since for that magazine.

The mark of the true priest was heavy on the Dean. The mark was on Quinlan; it was on Keefe. It was on every priest he could think of, including a few on the bum, and his good friend and bad companion, Father Desmond. But it was not on him, not properly. They, the others, were stained with it beyond all disguise or disfigurement—indelibly, as indeed Holy Orders by its sacramental nature must stain, for keeps in this world and the one to come. "Thou art a priest forever." With him, however, it was something else and less, a mask or badge which he could and did remove at will, a temporal part to be played, almost only a doctor's or lawyer's. They, the others, would be lost in any persecution. The mark would doom them. But he, if that *dies irae* ever came—and it was every plump seminarian's apple-cheeked dream—could pass as the most harmless and useful of humans, a mailman, a bus rider, a husband. But would he? No. They would see. I, he would say, appearing unsought before the judging rabble, am a priest, of the order of Melchizedech. Take me. I am ready. *Deo gratias.*

Father Burner got out the money to pay and honked his horn. The woman, coming for the bottle and tray, took his money without acknowledging the tip. She stood aside, the bottle held gingerly between offended fingers, final illustration of her lambishness, and watched him drive away. Father Burner, applying a cloven foot to the pedal, gave it the gas. He sensed the woman hoping in her simple heart to see him wreck the car and meet instant death in an unpostponed act of God.

Under the steadying influence of his stomach thrust against the wheel, the car proceeded while he searched himself for a cigarette. He passed a hitchhiker, saw him fade out of view in the mirror overhead, gesticulate wetly in the distance. Was the son of a gun thumbing his nose? Anticlericalism. But pray that your flight be not in the winter . . . No, wrong text: he would not run away.

The road skirted a tourist village. He wondered who stayed in those places and seemed to remember a story in one of the religious scandal sheets . . . ILLICIT LOVE in steaming red type.

A billboard cried out, "Get in the scrap and—get in the scrap!" Some of this advertising, he thought, was pretty slick. Put out probably by big New York and Chicago agencies with crack men on their staffs, fellows who had studied at *Time*. How would it be to write advertising? He knew a few things about layout and type faces from editing the parish paper. He had read somewhere about the best men of our time being in advertising, the air corps of business. There was room for better taste in the Catholic magazines, for someone with a name in the secular field to step in and drive out the money-changers with their trusses, corn cures, non-tangle rosary beads, and crosses that glow in the dark. It was a thought.

Coming into the city limits, he glanced at his watch, but neglected to notice the time. The new gold strap got his eye. The watch itself, a priceless pyx, held the hour (time is money) sacred, like a host. He had chosen it for an ordination gift rather than the usual chalice. It took the kind of courage he had to go against the grain there.

"I'm a dirty stinker!" Father Desmond flung his arms out hard against the mattress. His fists opened on the sheet, hungry for the spikes, meek and ready. "I'm a dirty stinker, Ernest!"

Father Burner, seated deep in a red leather chair at the sick man's bedside, crossed his legs forcefully. "Now don't take on so, Father."

"Don't call me 'Father'!" Father Desmond's eyes fluttered open momentarily, but closed again on the reality of it all. "I don't deserve it. I'm a disgrace to the priesthood! I am not worthy! Lord, Lord, I am not worthy!"

A nurse entered and stuck a thermometer in Father Desmond's mouth.

Father Burner smiled at the nurse. He lit a cigarette and wondered if she understood. The chart probably bore the diagnosis "pneumonia," but if she had been a nurse very long she would know all about that. She released Father Desmond's wrist and recorded his pulse on her pad. She took the thermometer and left the room.

Father Desmond surged up in bed and flopped, turning with a wrench of the covers, on his stomach. He lay gasping like a fish out of water. Father Burner could smell it on his breath yet.

"Do you want to go to confession?"

"No! I'm not ready for it. I want to remember this time!"

"Oh, all right." It was funny, if a little tiresome, the way the Irish could exaggerate a situation. They all had access to the same two or three emotions. They all played the same battered barrel organ handed down through generations. Dying, fighting, talking, drinking, praying . . . wakes, wars, politics, pubs, church. The fates were decimated and hamstrung among them. They loved monotony.

Father Desmond, doing the poor soul uttering his last words in italics, said: "We make too good a thing out of confession, Ernest! Ever think of that, Ernest?" He wagged a nicotined finger. Some of his self-contempt seemed to overshoot its mark and include Father Burner.

Father Burner honked his lips—*plutt!* "Hire a hall, Ed."

Father Desmond clawed a rosary out from under his pillow.

Father Burner left.

He put the car in the garage. On the way to his room he passed voices in the Dean's office.

"Father Burner!" the Dean called through the door.

Father Burner stayed in the hallway, only peeping in, indicating numerous commitments elsewhere. Quinlan and Keefe were with the Dean.

"Apparently, Father, you failed to kill yourself." Then, for Keefe, the Dean said, "Father Burner fulfills the dream of the American hierarchy and the principle of historical localization. He's been up in his flying machine all morning."

"I didn't go up." Sullenness came and went in his voice. "It rained." He shuffled one foot, about to leave, when the Dean's left eyebrow wriggled up, warning, holding him.

"I don't believe you've had the pleasure." The Dean gave Keefe to Father Burner. "Father Keefe, sir, went through school with Father Quinlan—from the grades through the priesthood." The Dean described an arc with his breviary, dripping with ribbons, to show the passing years. Father Burner nodded.

"Well?" The Dean frowned at Father Burner. "Has the cat got your tongue, sir? Why don't you be about greeting Father O'Keefe—or Keefe, is it?"

"Keefe," Keefe said.

Father Burner, caught in the old amber of his inadequacy, stepped over and shook Keefe's hand once.

Quinlan stood by and let the drama play itself out.

Keefe, smiling a curious mixture more anxiety than amusement, said, "It's a pleasure, Father."

"Same here," Father Burner said.

"Well, good day, sirs!" The Dean cracked open his breviary and began to read, lips twitching.

Father Burner waited for them in the hall. Before he could explain that he thought too much of the Dean not to humor him and that besides the old fool was out of his head, the Dean proclaimed after them, "The Chancery phoned, Father Burner. You will hear confessions there tonight. I suppose one of those Cathedral jokers lost his faculties."

Yes, Father Burner knew, it was common procedure all right for the Archbishop to confer promotions by private interview, but every time a priest got called to the Cathedral it did not mean simply that. Many received sermons and it was most likely now someone was needed to hear confessions. And still Father Burner, feeling his pocket, was glad he had not remembered to mail the letter. He would not bother to speak to Quinlan and Keefe now.

III. NIGHT

"And for your penance say five Our Fathers and five Hail Marys and pray for my intention. And now make a good act of contrition. *Misereatur tui omnipotens Deus dimissis peccatis tuis . . .*" Father Burner swept out into the current of the prayer, stroking strongly in Latin, while the penitent, a miserable boy coming into puberty, paddled as fast as he could along the shore in English.

Finishing first, Father Burner waited for the boy to conclude. When, breathless, he did, Father Burner anointed the air and shot a whisper, "God bless you," kicking the window shut with the heel of his hand, ejecting the boy, an ear of corn shucked clean, into the world again. There was nobody on the other side of the confessional, so Father Burner turned on the signal light. A big spider drowsy in

his web, drugged with heat and sins, he sat waiting for
the next one to be hurled into his presence by guilt ruddy
ripe, as with the boy, or, as with the old ladies who come
early and try to stay late, by the spiritual famine of their
lives or simply the desire to tell secrets in the dark.

He held his wrist in such a way as to see the sweat
gleaming in the hairs. He looked at his watch. He had been
at it since seven and now it was after nine. If there were no
more kneeling in his section of the Cathedral at 9:30 he
could close up and have a cigarette. He was too weary to
read his office, though he had the Little Hours, Vespers,
and Compline still to go. It was the last minutes in the
confessional that got him—the insensible end of the excur-
sion that begins with so many sinewy sensations and good
intentions to look sharp at the landscape. In the last minutes how many priests, would-be surgeons of the soul,
ended as blacksmiths, hammering out absolution anyway?

A few of the Cathedral familiars still drifted around the
floor. They were day and night in the shadows praying.
Meeting one of them, Father Burner always wanted to get
away. They were collectors of priests' blessings in a day
when most priests felt ashamed to raise their hands to God
outside the ceremonies. Their respect for a priest was fa-
natic, that of the unworldly, the martyrs, for an emissary
of heaven. They were so desperately disposed to death that
the manner of dying was their greatest concern. But Father
Burner had an idea there were more dull pretenders than
saints among them. They inspired no unearthly feelings in
him, as true sanctity was supposed to, and he felt it was
all right not to like them. They spoke of God, the Blessed
Virgin, of miracles, cures, and visitations, as of people and
items in the news, which was annoying. The Cathedral, because of its location, described by brokers as exclusive, was
not so much frequented by these wretches as it would
have been if more convenient to the slums. But nevertheless a few came there, like the diarrheic pigeons, also a
scandal to the neighborhood, and would not go away. Father Burner, from his glancing contact with them, had concluded that body odor is the real odor of sanctity.

Through the grating now Father Burner saw the young

Vicar General stop a little distance up the aisle and speak to a couple of people who were possible prospects for Father Burner. "Anyone desiring to go to confession should do so at once. In a few minutes the priests will be gone from the confessionals." He crossed to the other side of the Cathedral.

Father Burner did not like to compare his career with the Vicar General's. The Archbishop had taken the Vicar General, a younger man than Father Burner by at least fifteen years, direct from the seminary. After a period of trial as Chancellor, he was raised to his present eminence—for reasons much pondered by the clergy and more difficult to discern than those obviously accounted for by intelligence, appearance, and, post factum, the loyalty consequent upon his selection over many older and possibly abler men. It was a medieval act of preference, a slap in the face to the monsignori, a rebuke to the principle of advancement by years applied elsewhere. The Vicar General had the quality of inscrutability in an ideal measure. He did not seem at all given to gossip or conspiracy or even to that owlish secrecy peculiar to secretaries and so exasperating to others. He had possibly no enemies and certainly no intimates. In time he would be a bishop unless, as was breathed wherever the Cloth gathered over food and drink, he really was "troubled with sanctity," which might lead to anything else, the cloister or insanity.

The Vicar General appeared at the door of Father Burner's compartment. "The Archbishop will see you, Father, before you leave tonight." He went up the aisle, genuflected before the main altar, opened as a gate one of the host of brass angels surrounding the sanctuary, and entered the sacristies.

Before he would let hope have its way with him, Father Burner sought to recast the expression on the Vicar General's face. He could recall nothing significant. Very probably there had been nothing to see. Then, with a rush, he permitted himself to think this was his lucky day. Already he was formulating the way he would let the news out, providing he decided not to keep it a secret for a time. He might do that. It would be delicious to go about his business until the very last minute, to savor the old aggravations and feel none of the sting, to receive the old quips and smiles with good grace and know them to be toothless. The news, once out, would fly through the diocese. Hear about Burner at Saint Pat's, Tom? Finally landed himself a parish. Yeah, I just had it from McKenna. So I guess the A. B. wasn't so sore at the Round One after all. Well, he's just ornery enough to make a go of it.

Father Burner, earlier in the evening, had smoked a cigarette with one of the young priests attached to the Cathedral (a classmate of Quinlan's but not half the prig), stalling, hoping someone would come and say the Archbishop wanted to see him. When nothing happened except the usual small talk and introductions to a couple of missionaries stopping over, he had given up hope easily. He had seen the basis for his expectations as folly once more. It did not bother him after the fact was certain. He was amenable to any kind of finality. He had a light heart for a Ger—an American of German descent. And his hopes rose higher each time and with less cause. He was a ball that bounced up only. He had kept faith. And now—his just reward.

A little surprised he had not thought of her first, he admitted his mother into the new order of things. He wanted to open the letter from her, still in his coat, and late as it was send her a wire, which would do her more good than a night's sleep. He thought of himself back in her kitchen, home from the sem for the holidays, a bruiser in a tight black suit, his feet heavy on the oven door. She was fussing at the stove and he was promising her a porcelain one as big as a house after he got his parish. But he let her know, kidding on the square, that he would be running things at the rectory. It would not be the old story of the priest taking orders from his housekeeper, even if she was his mother (seminarians, from winter evenings of shooting the bull, knew only too well the pitfalls of parish life), or as with Ed Desmond a few years ago when his father was still living with him, the old man losing his marbles one by one, butting in when people came for advice and instructions, finally coming to believe he was the one to say Mass in his son's absence—no need to get a strange priest in—and sneaking into the box to hear confessions the day before they took him away.

He would be gentle with his mother, however, even if she talked too much, as he recalled she did the last time he saw her. She was well-preserved and strong for her age and ought to be able to keep the house up. Once involved in the social life of the parish she could be a valuable agent in coping with any lay opposition, which was too often the case when a new priest took over.

He resolved to show no nervousness before the Archbishop. A trifle surprised, yes—the Archbishop must have his due—but not overly affected by good fortune. If questioned, he would display a lot of easy confidence not unaccompanied by a touch of humility, a phrase or two like "God willing" or "with the help of Almighty God and your prayers, Your Excellency." He would also not forget to look the part—reliable, casual, cool, an iceberg, only the tip of his true worth showing.

At precisely 9:30 Father Burner picked up his breviary and backed out of the stall. But then there was the scuff of a foot and the tap of one of the confessional doors closing and then, to tell him the last penitent was a woman, the scent of apple blossoms. He turned off the light, saying "Damn!" to himself, and sat down again inside. He threw back the partition and led off, "Yes?" He placed his hand alongside his head and listened, looking down into the deeper darkness of his cassock sleeve.

"I . . ."

"Yes?" At the heart of the apple blossoms another scent bloomed: gin and vermouth.

"Bless me, Father, I . . . have sinned."

Father Burner knew this kind. They would always wait until the last moment. How they managed to get themselves into church at all, and then into the confessional, was a mystery. Sometimes liquor thawed them out. This one was evidently young, nubile. He had a feeling it was going to be adultery. He guessed it was up to him to get her under way.

"How long since your last confession?"

"I don't know . . ."

"Have you been away from the Church?"

"Yes."

"Are you married?"

"Yes."

"To a Catholic?"

"No."

"Protestant?"

"No."

"Jew?"

"No."

"Atheist?"

"No—nothing."

"Were you married by a priest?"

"Yes."

"How long ago was that?"

"Four years."

"Any children?"

"No."

"Practice birth control?"

"Yes, sometimes."

"Don't you know it's a crime against nature and the Church forbids it?"

"Yes."

"Don't you know that France fell because of birth control?"

"No."

"Well, it did. Was it your husband's fault?"

"You mean—the birth control?"

"Yes."

"Not wholly."

"And you've been away from the Church ever since your marriage?"

"Yes."

"Now you see why the Church is against mixed marriages. All right, go on. What else?"

"I don't know . . ."

"Is that what you came to confess?"

"No. Yes. I'm sorry, I'm afraid that's all."

"Do you have a problem?"

"I think that's all, Father."

"Remember, it is your obligation, and not mine, to ex-amine your conscience. The task of instructing persons with regard to these delicate matters—I refer to the connubial relationship—is not an easy one. Nevertheless, since there is a grave obligation imposed by God, it cannot be shirked. If you have a problem——"

"I don't have a *problem*."

"Remember, God never commands what is impossible and so if you make use of the sacraments regularly you have every reason to be confident that you will be able to overcome this evil successfully, with His help. I hope this is all clear to you."

"All clear."

"Then if you are heartily sorry for your sins for your penance say the rosary daily for one week and remember it is the law of the Church that you attend Mass on Sundays and holy days and receive the sacraments at least once a year. It's better to receive them often. Ask your pastor about birth control if it's still not clear to you. Or read a Catholic book on the subject. And now make a good act of contrition . . ."

Father Burner climbed the three flights of narrow stairs. He waited a moment in silence, catching his breath. He knocked on the door and was suddenly afraid its density prevented him from being heard and that he might be found standing there like a fool or a spy. But to knock again, if heard the first time, would seem importunate.

"Come in, Father."

At the other end of the long study the Archbishop sat behind an ebony desk. Father Burner waited before him as though expecting not to be asked to sit down. The only light in the room, a lamp on the desk, was so set that it kept the Archbishop's face in the dark, fell with a gentle sparkle upon his pectoral cross, and was absorbed all around by the fabric of the piped cloth he wore. Father Burner's eyes came to rest upon the Archbishop's freckled hand—ringed, square, and healthy.

"Be seated, Father."

"Thank you, Your Excellency."

"Oh, sit in this chair, Father." There were two chairs. Father Burner changed to the soft one. He had a suspicion that in choosing the other one he had fallen into a silly trap, that it was a game the Archbishop played with his visitors: the innocent ones, seeing no issue, would take the soft chair, because handier; the guilty would go a step out of their way to take the hard one. "I called Saint Patrick's this morning, Father, but you were . . . out."

"I was visiting Father Desmond, Your Excellency."

"Father Desmond . . ."

"He's in the hospital."

"I know. Friend of his, are you, Father?"

"No, Your Excellency. Well"—Father Burner waited for the cock to crow the third time—"yes, I *know* the man." At once he regretted the scriptural complexion of the words and wondered if it were possible for the Archbishop not to be thinking of the earlier betrayal.

"It was good of you to visit Father Desmond, especially since you are not close to him. I hope he is better, Father."

"He is, Your Excellency."

The Archbishop got up and went across the room to a cabinet. "Will you have a little glass of wine, Father?"

"No. No, thanks, Your Excellency." Immediately he realized it could be another trap and, if so, he was caught again.

"Then I'll have a drop . . . *solus.*" The Archbishop poured a glass and brought it back to the desk. "A little wine for the stomach's sake, Father."

Father Burner, not sure what he was expected to say to that, nodded gravely and said, "Yes, Your Excellency." He had seen that the Archbishop wore carpet slippers and that they had holes in both toes.

"But perhaps you've read Saint Bernard, Father, and recall where he says we priests remember well enough the apostolic counsel to use wine, but overlook the adjective 'little.'"

"I must confess I haven't read Saint Bernard lately, Your Excellency." Father Burner believed this was somehow in his favor. "Since seminary, in fact."

"Not all priests, Father, have need of him. A hard saint . . . for hardened sinners. What is your estimate of Saint Paul?"

Father Burner felt familiar ground under his feet at last. There were the Pauline and Petrine factions—a futile business, he thought—but he knew where the Archbishop stood and exclaimed, "One of the greatest——"

"Really! So many young men today consider him . . . a bore. It's always the deep-breathing ones, I notice. They say he cuts it too fine."

"I've never thought so, Your Excellency."

"Indeed? Well, it's a question I like to ask my priests. Perhaps you knew that."

"No, I didn't, Your Excellency."

"So much the better then . . . but I see you appraising the melodeon, Father. Are you musical?"

"Not at all, Your Excellency. Violin lessons as a child." Father Burner laughed quickly, as though it were nothing.

"But you didn't go on with them?"

"No, Your Excellency." He did not mean it to sound as sad as it came out.

"What a pity."

"No great loss, Your Excellency."

"You are too . . . modest, Father. But perhaps the violin was not your instrument."

"I guess it wasn't, Your Excellency." Father Burner laughed out too loud.

"And you have the choir at Saint Patrick's, Father?"

"Not this year, Your Excellency. Father Quinlan has it."

"Now I recall . . ."

"Yes." So far as he was concerned—and there were plenty of others who thought so, too—Quinlan had played hell with the choir, canning all the women, some of them members for fifteen and twenty years, a couple even longer and practically living for it, and none of them as bad as Quinlan said. The liturgical stuff that Quinlan tried to pull off was all right in monasteries, where they had the time to train for it, but in a parish it sounded stodgy to ears used to the radio and split up the activity along sexual

lines, which was really old hat in the modern world. The
Dean liked it though. He called it "honest" and eulogized
the men from the pulpit—not a sign that he heard how
they brayed and whinnied and just gave out or failed to
start—and each time it happened ladies in the congregation
were sick and upset for days afterward, for he inevitably
ended by attacking women, pants, cocktails, communism,
cigarettes, and running around half naked. The women
looked at the men in the choir, all pretty in surplices, and
said to themselves they knew plenty about some of them
and what they had done to some women.

"He's tried a little Gregorian, hasn't he—Father Quinlan?"

"Yes, Your Excellency," Father Burner said. "He has."

"Would you say it's been a success—or perhaps I should
ask you first if you care for Gregorian, Father."

"Oh, yes, Your Excellency. Very much."

"Many, I know, don't . . . I've been told our chant
sounds like a wild bull in a red barn or consumptives coughing into a bottle, but I will have it in the Cathedral, Father.
Other places, I am aware, have done well with . . . light
opera."

Father Burner frowned.

"We are told the people prefer and understand it. But
at the risk of seeming reactionary, a fate my office prevents
me from escaping in any event, I say we spend more time
listening to the voice of the people than is good for either
it or us. We have been too generous with our ears, Father.
We have handed over our tongues also. When they are restored to us I wonder if we shall not find our ears more
itching than before and our tongues more tied than ever."

Father Burner nodded in the affirmative.

"We are now entering the whale's tail, Father. We must
go back the way we came in." The Archbishop lifted the
lid of the humidor on the desk. "Will you smoke, Father?"

"No, thanks, Your Excellency."

The Archbishop let the lid drop. "Today there are few
saints, fewer sinners, and everybody is already saved. We
are all heroes in search of an underdog. As for villains, the
classic kind with no illusions about themselves, they are

. . . extinct. The very devil, for instance—where the devil
is the devil today, Father?"

Father Burner, as the Archbishop continued to look at
him, bit his lips for the answer, secretly injured that he
should be expected to know, bewildered even as the children he toyed with in catechism.

The Archbishop smiled, but Father Burner was not sure
at what—whether at him or what had been said. "Did you
see, Father, where our brother Bishop Buckles said Hitler
remains the one power on earth against the Church?"

Yes, Father Burner remembered seeing it in the paper; it
was the sort of thing that kept Quinlan talking for days.
"I did, Your Excellency."

"Alas, poor Buckles! He's a better croquet player than
that." The Archbishop's hands unclasped suddenly and fell
upon his memo pad. He tore off about a week and seemed
to feel better for it. His hands, with no hint of violence
about them now, came together again. "We look hard to
the right and left, Father. It is rather to the center, I think,
we should look—to ourselves, the devil in us."

Father Burner knew the cue for humility when he heard
it. "Yes, Your Excellency."

With his chubby fingers the Archbishop made a steeple
that was more like a dome. His eyes were reading the memo.
"For instance, Father, I sometimes appear at banquets—
when they can't line up a good foreign correspondent—banquets at which the poor are never present and at which I
am unfailingly confronted by someone exceedingly well off
who is moved to inform me that 'religion' is a great consolation to him. Opium, rather, I always think, perhaps wrong-
fully and borrowing a word from one of our late competi-
tors, which is most imprudent of me, a bishop."

The Archbishop opened a drawer and drew out a sheet of
paper and an envelope. "Yes, the rich have souls," he said
softly, answering an imaginary objection which happened to
be Father Burner's. "But if Christ were really with them
they would not be themselves—that is to say, rich."

"Very true, Your Excellency," Father Burner said.

The Archbishop faced sideways to use an old typewriter. "And likewise, lest we forget, we would not be our-

selves, that is to say—what? For we square the circle beautifully in almost every country on earth. We bring neither peace nor a sword. The rich give us money. We give them consolation and make of the eye of the needle a gate. Together we try to reduce the Church, the Bride of Christ, to a streetwalker." The Archbishop rattled the paper, Father Burner's future, into place and rolled it crookedly into the typewriter. "Unfortunately for us, it doesn't end there. The penance will not be shared so equitably. Your Christian name, Father, is——?"

"Ernest, Your Excellency."

The Archbishop typed several words and stopped, looking over at Father Burner. "I can't call to mind a single Saint Ernest, Father. Can you help me?"

"There were two, I believe, Your Excellency, but Butler leaves them out of his *Lives*."

"They would be German saints, Father?"

"Yes, Your Excellency. There was one an abbot and the other an archbishop."

"If Butler had been Irish, as the name has come to indicate, I'd say that's an Irishman for you, Father. He does not forget to include a power of Irish saints." The Archbishop was Irish himself. Father Burner begged to differ with him, believing here was a wrong deliberately set up for him to right. "I am not Irish myself, Your Excellency, but some of my best friends are."

"Tut, tut, Father. Such tolerance will be the death of you." The Archbishop, typing a few words, removed the paper, signed it and placed it in the envelope. He got up and took down a book from the shelves. He flipped it open, glanced through several pages and returned it to its place. "No Ernests in Baring-Gould either. Well, Father, it looks as if you have a clear field."

The Archbishop came from behind the desk and Father Burner, knowing the interview was over, rose. The Archbishop handed him the envelope. Father Burner stuffed it hastily in his pocket and knelt, the really important thing, to kiss the Archbishop's ring and receive his blessing. They walked together toward the door.

"Do you care for pictures, Father?"

"Oh, yes, Your Excellency."

The Archbishop, touching him lightly on the arm, stopped before a reproduction of Raphael's Sistine Madonna. "There is a good peasant woman, Father, and a nice fat baby." Father Burner nodded his appreciation. "She could be Our Blessed Mother, Father, though I doubt it. There is no question about the baby. He is not Christ." The Archbishop moved to another picture. "Rembrandt had the right idea, Father. See the gentleman pushing Christ up on the cross? That is Rembrandt, a self-portrait." Father Burner thought of some of the stories about the Archbishop, that he slept on a cot, stood in line with the people sometimes to go to confession, that he fasted on alternate days the year round. Father Burner was thankful for such men as the Archbishop. "But here is Christ, Father." This time it was a glassy-eyed Christ whose head lay against the rough wood of the cross he was carrying. "That is Christ, Father. The Greek painted Our Saviour."

The Archbishop opened the door for Father Burner, saying, "And, Father, you will please not open the envelope until after your Mass tomorrow."

Father Burner went swiftly down the stairs. Before he got into his car he looked up at the Cathedral. He could scarcely see the cross glowing on the dome. It seemed as far away as the stars. The cross needed a brighter light or the dome ought to be painted gold and lit up like the state capitol, so people would see it. He drove a couple of blocks down the street, pulled up to the curb, opened the envelope, which had not been sealed, and read: "You will report on August 8 to the Reverend Michael Furlong, to begin your duties on that day as his assistant. I trust that in your new appointment you will find not peace but a sword."

ABOUT THE AUTHOR

J.F. Powers is the author of three collections of short stories—*Prince of Darkness* (1947), *The Presence of Grace* (1956), and *Look How The Fish Live* (1975)—and one novel, *Morte D'Urban* (1962), which won the National Book Award. He lives in Minnesota.